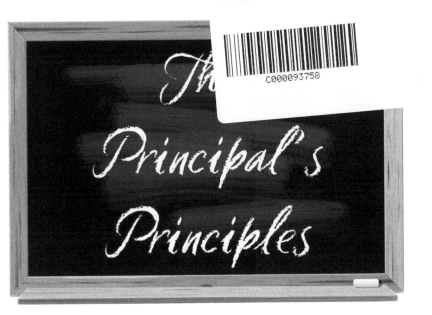

The Principal's Principles

by Tyler Wittkofksy

Tea With Coffee
— Media —

To MaMa,

As I pen down these words, my heart overflows with gratitude and love for the extraordinary woman who inspired it all—Wanda, the resilient and groundbreaking protagonist of "The Principal's Principles." Though a work of fiction, Wanda's journey mirrors the indomitable spirit and unwavering determination that you, my beloved MaMa, exhibited as the first female principal in Brunswick County, North Carolina, in 1987.

In the quiet corners of my imagination, Wanda's character takes shape, guided by the echoes of your courage and the trailblazing path you paved. As I weave this tale of triumph against the backdrop of a rural community, I know that every obstacle Wanda faces is a testament to the challenges you conquered, the glass ceilings you shattered, and the lives you touched.

You, MaMa, are the heartbeat of this narrative. Through the lens of fiction, I strive to capture the essence of your strength, your compassion, and your unwavering commitment to education. From the early days when I sat in your office, pencil in hand, to the moments when you encouraged me to embark on this writing journey during that unforgettable winter of 2018, your influence has been the ink that colors every page.

As I embark on this literary journey, I carry with me the gift of your inspiration, the echo of your encouragement, and the profound impact you've had on my life. The miles stretch between us as Gracie and I traverse the United States cannot diminish the closeness we share, the countless phone calls that bridge the distance, or the depth of gratitude I feel.

Thank you, MaMa, for being not only the first female principal but also my best friend, mentor, and the unwavering force behind my writer's pen. Your belief in me, your support through every twist and turn, and your cheers for my sometimes outlandish dreams have been the wind beneath my wings.

As "The Principal's Principles" finds its way into the hands of readers, know that every word is a tribute to you—a woman whose impact reaches far beyond the pages of a book. You are the embodiment of strength, resilience, and love, and I am forever blessed to be your grandchild.

With love and profound gratitude,

Contents

Chapter 1

The Summer of '87

Wanda Hare tipped the mason jar glass full of sweet tea to her lips as she sat in the rocking chair on the back porch. With the bright sun beating down on her fair skin, she brushed her wavy black hair from her face. Wanda was newly thirty and had begun her career teaching ten years ago at twenty, straight out of graduation from the University of North Carolina at Wilmington. She had worked hard to graduate early from college, thanks to her dedication and preparation.

Ever since she was a young girl in elementary school, she aspired to teach and help to educate people. So many of her teachers had affected her, and she wanted to do the same for others.

Wanda glanced across her yard to find her husband, George, leaning against a hoe and the wad of chewing tobacco causing a bulge in his cheek. George was your typical country boy who grew up farming and continued once he finished school. Wanda reminisced about when she and her husband were younger, as she admired his military-style haircut and dark, leathery skin.

George was a few years the elder of Wanda and was a few grades ahead of her growing up. Wanda recalled an incident where George, who had a reputation for being a troublemaker and class clown, left a dead rat in his teacher's desk. Wanda chuckled; it was ironic that she - an English teacher with a passion for education - had married a country boy with a disdain for schooling.

As Wanda took another sip of sweet tea from her glass, she saw her nine-year-old daughter, Michelle, run up to her dad and jump into his arms. She was an adorable girl with long black hair that danced in the wind as she ran, her eyes lighting up the room and never without a smile. Michelle loved to help her dad in the fields, planting and hoeing the crops for the upcoming seasons. She was a tomboy.

The phone rang, interrupting Wanda's thoughts and prompting her to rush inside to answer it.

"Hello?" Wanda answered as she lifted the phone off the receiver and carefully placed it against her ear, trying not to get tangled in the cord.

"Wanda, this is Shawn Carlile," a man's booming voice echoed from the other end of the line. Shawn Carlile was the newest superintendent of the school district Wanda taught in. He achieved a historic milestone in their system by being the first African American to serve as assistant principal, principal, and superintendent. All by the time he was in his forties.

"Well, hello Shawn! How are you?" Wanda asked.

"I'm doing well, thank you," Shawn said as he paused for a moment. He cleared his throat. "Wanda, do you have a minute to talk?"

Wanda's mind instantly wandered, thinking about what Shawn might want to talk about on a Saturday afternoon. "Sure thing, Shawn," Wanda finally said as she made her way to her chair.

"Wanda, I'm making some serious changes throughout our school district," he started. Wanda's thoughts became more vicarious as her heart dropped and she feared what would come next. "You know things are finally changing. I'm breaking stereotypes and defying the odds. I want to break another one, with your help. You should be the first female principal in our school district."

Wanda sat in silence, amazement, joy, and then worry. How would they receive her, being a female? How would her life change? What did she need to do? She finally found the right words to say. "What do I need to do, Shawn?"

"I'm going to assume that means you're accepting the position," he laughed back. "Nothing except get your master's degree in educational leadership within four years of starting the position, Wanda. Of course, the school district will pay for a portion of it. You can work on it through the next few years. The job is yours when you're ready."

"Shawn," Wanda began, as her mind instantly assumed. "You're not promoting me *because* I'm a woman, are you?" she cautiously finished.

"Oh, Heavens no, Wanda!" Shawn said, half insulted and half stunned. "Wanda, you are the most qualified educator in our system. You have been serving as Vice Principal at East Holcomb for the last three years, and honestly, you should have been promoted years ago. Unfortunately, our district has been slow to change," Shawn said, expressing his frustration with the district's slow progress. He finished, more clearly and calmly than he began.

Wanda felt bad about questioning Shawn's decision. "Thank you, Shawn," she whispered. "Just making sure. I want to earn what I get, and need to ensure I deserve it. However, I appreciate your kind words." As she finished the sentence, Wanda's husband George walked into the house, sensing his wife's mood. "Can I have a few days to think about it, Shawn?"

"Absolutely, Wanda." Shawn said. "Think about where you want to go to college. I hear App State is a good choice for educational leadership."

Shawn and Wanda said their goodbyes as Wanda slowly placed the phone back on the receiver. She looked over at her husband and daughter, who had just pranced through the back door behind her father.

"Mommy, what's wrong?" Michelle said, almost sounding like she was singing the words to her question.

George rested his hand on Michelle's wavy black hair that matched her mother's and said to her in his strong country accent, "Chelle, I don't reckon there's a thing wrong witchur Mama. In fact, I reckon there's somethin' good 'bout to come out 'er mouth."

"They offered me Shawn's Principal job," Wanda said, still staring into the receiver of the phone, stunned.

Michelle, not knowing if that was a good thing or not, looked up at her dad. She knew she didn't like the principal at her school because he was always mean and getting people in trouble. Maybe her mother's school was different? "What's that mean, Daddy?" she whispered, tugging slightly on his sleeve that was dangling above her head.

"It means your Mama's gettin' ready to have 'r dreams come true," he smiled back at her.

Michelle wasn't sure how her mother's dream could be of being a principal. The girl knew that her own dreams normally made her happy, so she was therefore happy for her mother.

She slipped from under her dad's rough hand and ran into the coolness of her mother's arms. "YAY! I'm so happy for you, Mommy!" she shouted as her arms wrapped tightly around her mother's waist and face buried in her stomach.

"Go ahead up to your room and play, Sweetie, so me and Daddy can talk," Wanda said, looking down happily at her daughter and then back up with worry to her husband.

Michelle, sensing the worry and noticing the unconvincing smile her mother gave her, quickly made her way to the stairs. As she made her way up the steps, she stopped at the top. She was just out of sight to where anyone could see her, but close enough that she could still hear her parents talking. It wasn't her first time eavesdropping on her parents.

"'Swrong Wanda? Ain't this whatcha been wantin'?" George asked when Michelle was out of sight.

"Yes George, it is. But," Wanda stopped and looked down at the phone again.

"But what?" George called back, more worried now.

"George, I'm worried about the backlash," Wanda said quietly, so quietly in fact that Michelle had to strain her ears just to hear her clearly. Michelle wasn't sure what 'backlash' was, but she knew it didn't sound good.

"Whatcha mean, dear?" George worriedly asked, as his voice came closer to his wife. Now Michelle knew that 'backlash' wasn't good at all. She could always tell in her dad's voice when something worried him, he wasn't great at hiding it. Michelle put her ear closer to the bottom of the wall, propping herself up with one arm underneath and one bracing the wall.

"Shawn faced a lot of disrespect and criticism as the first African American superintendent. And not just from students, but also from the principals in the district. He was called names I cannot even repeat, George. I'm worried about Michelle more than anything," Wanda finished.

Michelle sat in her bed, with her knees tucked to her chest, tears slowly sliding sideways from her eyes. She was worried about her mother. She thought being a principal was what her mother had always dreamed, but now Michelle felt like she was getting in her mother's way.

As she sat in her room, she heard footsteps approaching from the stairs. She relaxed her knees, wiped her eyes, and laid her head down on the pillow, facing away from the doorway. She sniffled her nose one time before whichever one of her parents coming down the hallway could reach her room.

"'Chelle?" her dad called out from the doorway.

"Yes, Daddy?" she replied softly.

"You okay?"

"Yes, Daddy," she said unconvincingly.

She heard her dad walking towards the end of her bed, where he sat down and laid his hand on her leg. "You heard me an' yer Mama, didn'tcha?" he asked her.

Michelle hesitated for a minute before answering, "I did. Daddy, I don't want Mommy to not take this new job because of me. I know this is what she wants more than anything! Daddy, please make sure she takes it!"

"Hunny, lis'en. Your Mama ain't gonna turn this job down 'cause-a you. In fact, I don't reckon she'll turn it down a'tall. There's a lotta grownup stuff involved in this here decision, stuff you can't understand. Me an' your Mama love you to death 'Chelle. Everythang we do is for you, baby."

Michelle sat up and wrapped her arms around her dad's chest, squeezing him tightly. She rested her head on his arm as he reached around and rubbed her head. She felt at peace like this, like everything would be okay.

The next morning, Wanda left her house and began walking to her parents' house. She and George lived right down the street from her parents, which made visits to their house a regular occurrence. As she made her way down the dirt road they lived on, she couldn't help but let her mind escape reality and imagine what it would be like to finally be the principal.

"Good morning students, this is Principal Wanda," She would start off the morning announcements. She would be the type of principal who wanted to make the students feel comfortable and let them know she was approachable and would go above and beyond for them.

"Today's lunch menu will consist of chicken nuggets, mashed potatoes, and green beans with a roll. Don't forget, there will be a basketball game tonight against North Holcomb High School. Be sure you come out and support YOUR East Holcomb Panthers!" She was an avid basketball fan and couldn't wait to help raise attendance at sporting events. She wanted to make the Panther Pride even more clear across Holcomb County.

After the thought of the morning announcements, her mind wandered to the basketball game. She was watching the game in the student section, laughing and talking with the students. She felt like she was fitting in well with the students, like they accepted her despite being a woman.

As Wanda arrived at her parents' house, she saw their small dachshund, Cashew, running around outside. Cashew was a chubby dog, nearly five years old now. He was a light brown color with a white underbelly. The unique thing, perhaps, was the purple spots that littered his tongue. Wanda loved the purple spots; they added spunk to his already unique character.

"Come here, Cashew," Wanda said as she walked into the yard and bent down, hands on her knees and clicking her tongue against her teeth to get his attention. With his tongue hanging out the side of his mouth, Cashew came running to Wanda at the sound of her voice. He leaped up and knocked her down as he began giving her slobbery kisses.

"Okay, okay, okay," Wanda laughed as she put her hands over her face to protect it from the spotted tongue of Cashew.

"Cashew, come here boy!" Wanda's dad, Josiah, called in his soft and caring voice from the door of his house. Josiah's slight frame leaned against the door as he spit a wad of chewing tobacco out. He ran his hand across his bare head and rubbed the little stubble on his small and pointed face.

Wanda looked up and caught her daddy's stare. His eyes really set him apart-they were the most prominent sky-blue people had ever seen. He had gained the nick-name Ol' Blue among the locals in the county because of his eyes.

Cashew leaped off Wanda and ran towards Josiah, sitting promptly next to him as he got to his feet. Wanda made her way off the ground and towards her parents' house to greet her dad. "How are you today, Daddy?" Wanda asked as she hugged Josiah.

"I'm good Hunny, how're you?" He smiled, wrapping his small arms around her.

"I have great news," Wanda chirped as she embraced her daddy's hug. "Is Momma here?"

"She sure is. Let me get her," he said as he let go of the embrace and disappeared into the house.

Wanda followed in behind him, making her way into the living room of her childhood home. As she walked through the hallway, she glanced at the various pictures of her, her and George, and her, George, and Michelle. She stopped and looked at one picture: the picture of her giving the Valedictorian speech at her high school graduation held her gaze. She was the first female Vale-dictorian at East Holcomb High, something she had been so proud of. Something her parents had been so proud of.

Her hand reached for the picture, as if trying to revive the memories of her parents' joyful smiles. She wanted to tell the captivating story and give the speech she gave to the audience once more. To be surrounded by the standing ovation after the speech, one led by her parents. It was one of the proudest moments of her life, second only to the birth of Michelle. Would accepting the principal position top being Valedictorian?

"What're you doing, Hunny?" Josiah asked as he and JoAnne came around the corner. JoAnne and Wanda often got mistaken for sisters rather than mother and daughter.

"Walking down memory lane," Wanda smiled as she finished her reminiscing and resumed her journey to the living room.

The three made their way into the living room and took their seats. "Well, Hunny, what's the good news for me and your Momma?" Josiah said.

Wanda smiled and rubbed her hands together, "I got offered the position as Principal at East Holcomb. The superintendent, Shawn Carlile, you know Shawn, right Daddy? Sure, you do. Well, he called me and offered me the position."

"Did you take it, Sweetheart?" JoAnne asked, smiling and clapping her hands silently.

"Not yet Momma," Wanda quietly whispered. She looked away from her parents, almost ashamed of her answer.

"Hunny," Josiah started. "Why not?"

"Daddy, I'm afraid of what will happen," she confessed, avoiding her parents' caring gaze to prevent herself from being influenced by them. "I mean, being the first female principal in the district, how are people going to take that? How will people treat me? How will people treat Michelle?"

"Hunny, I'ma tell you one thing," Josiah said as he reached over to hold JoAnne's hand. "You were the first female Valedictorian, and you never worried one bit about that. I know you're worried right now about Michelle, but Hunny, this is going to make a better future for her. She gets to see her Mama breaking down barriers. She will grow up knowing she can do anything she puts her mind to. Accept the position for her."

"Shawn Carlile," the voice from the other side of the receiver answered.

"Shawn, Wanda here," Wanda started, almost nervously chattering. "Did I catch you at a good time?"

"Wanda! Good to hear from you. Of course, of course," he responded. "To what do I owe the pleasure of speaking with you this evening?"

"I want to go to Wake Forest for my master's degree," she said, as she felt a smile cross her face.

Shawn let out an exhale of breath in relief. "Does this mean you're taking the position as Principal of East Holcomb?"

"Yes," Wanda said with a grin "Yes, it does."

"Wonderful!" Shawn couldn't hide the excitement trickling from his voice. "If I may ask, what made you decide?"

"I want to do it for my daughter."

Chapter 2

The First Day

W anda walked into her new office for the first time. The office was almost as large as the last classroom she taught in, but better lit. She reached over and felt the dustiness that was her new light switch. As the lights turned on, Wanda saw the room clearly. It was her reward for working hard and overcoming obstacles to make her daughter proud.

Wanda carried a box full of decorations, notes, pictures, and teaching tools she'd collected during her ten years of teaching. She sat the box on the dusty mahogany desk and sank into the new chair. As she closed her eyes, she smiled and thought *"Michelle would have so much fun spinning around in this chair."* Wanda cherished her first moments in her new office, thinking of her daughter's beautiful hair spinning.

Her concentration was broken as the phone blared to life, startling Wanda out of her chair. Now standing, she reached down and answered the phone, "East Holcomb High, this is Wanda speaking."

"How's it goin' there, Principal?" George's strong southern accent boomed through the speaker.

"George! I just got here!" she laughed.

"You spun 'round in that big fancy chair yet?"

"Only once for Michelle," Wanda said with a giggle. "George, this is my dream. I have finally made it. After ten years, they recognized me for all my work."

"Oh Hunny, I know it, and I'm so prouda ya. You make me more an' more proud ev'ryday. I jus' wanted to call in and check on ya, see how you wasa settling in. I'ma letchu go and I'ma get back to tendin' the garden."

"George, I just love you to the moon and back! Have a good day and I can't wait to get home to tell you all about my day."

As Wanda placed the phone back down on the receiver, she heard a knock at her door. "Come in," she called back.

A tall man, at least 6'4, slowly pushed the closed door open to reveal his chiseled face. He ran a hand through his slicked back red hair and his forest green eyes shone in the light. "How are you doing this morning, Wanda? Or should I say Principal Hare," the man said as his tall frame snaked between the door and door frame and fully into the office.

"I don't want any special treatment. It's still Wanda, Robert," she laughed. Robert Kane and she had been teaching together for seven years before they were both promoted to Assistant Principal three years ago. He had made an enormous difference in the school, proving to be the backbone of administration and someone the students could trust. Robert had always encouraged her and praised her teaching methods when they taught together. "How can I help you this morning?"

"I just wanted to check in and see how you are settling in." With a comforting smile, Robert reminded her, "Don't forget that I'm your friend and I'm here to support you through this challenging transition."

"Thank you, Robert. I'm going to be honest with you. I'm a bit worried about the backlash I may face from some of the staff for being a woman. The school is still plagued by the old mindset. I want to ensure fair treatment for everyone and, most importantly, create a welcoming environment that enables our students to learn," Wanda said as she sat back down in her chair.

"Wanda, you know I'm here to support you. I'll back you at every turn. And I'll be 100% honest with you."

Wanda smiled and said, "Thank you Robert, our friendship is incredibly important to me."

Robert slid his body back out the door, pulling it shut behind him. Wanda arose and made her way to the door. As she reached out for the handle, she thought to herself, *"I want to make my staff and faculty to know I'm always available. I want to earn their trust. An open-door policy is the best thing for that."* She pushed gently on the door handle, opening the door quietly. She picked up a door stop and wedged it between the door and the ground to prevent anyone from closing it back.

Wanda strolled the empty halls of East Holcomb, her keys following her against the lockers, clacking on every one. School hadn't begun yet, so she wanted to make her way around and learn where everything was and belonged. She knew her way around the English wing, but wasn't all too familiar with some of the other wings. Faculty wasn't required to be at school yet, so it was eerily quiet today.

As she made her way down the halls, she paused. She cocked her head to the side, squinted her eyes, and turned her ears as she listened carefully. The *sch sch sch* of a piece of chalk on a chalkboard faintly flowed down the hallway. Looking ahead with her eyes still squinted, Wanda saw a classroom just down the hall with a light on. She made her way towards the light, her curiosity getting the best of her as she got closer to the door. *"Which teacher would be here now?"* she wondered to herself. Wanda had always arrived at school before the rest of the faculty, because she loved decorating her classroom with many literary themes. However, she had always been alone for the first few days.

As she approached the door and snuck her head through the doorframe, she found the shimmering bald head of the football coach - known to staff, faculty, and students alike as Coach - writing away while he watched game footage. Coach was a short and stout man, what he lacked with his 5'4 height he made up for in muscle mass. Wanda and Coach had not always seen eye to eye. Coach cared about his truck, his players, and the football program. He got confrontational with Wanda when one of his players would be failing her class in the past. Wanda did not back down and stood her ground because her priority was to ensure the students were learning. She didn't like it when students had a failing grade, but she knew it would often light a fire under them to do better. Coach, however, believed that his players should be given an educational pass since they brought so much money into the school system.

"Good afternoon, Coach," Wanda said as the rest of her body made its way through the door frame.

Coach, who had not noticed Wanda until she spoke, quickly paused the game footage and looked over at her. "Afternoon, Prince," he said coldly, in his stern and booming voice.

"Please, Coach, it's still Wanda. What're you doing here so early? Faculty doesn't have to report to school until next week."

"What does it look like I'm doing?" he said as he pointed the remote towards the boxy TV sitting on the cart on the other side of his classroom. "I'm preparing for our homecoming game. The boys are going to be prepared for Marcus Hankins High. Are you going to be there, or are you too good to show up?"

Wanda could tell Coach was going to be a problem for her for the rest of the school year. He was already disrespecting her, talking down to her, and it was only the first day. She didn't understand why he was acting like this... or did she? "Coach, of course I'll be there. I will be at every home game this season and I'll try to make as many away games as possible. I love my students and want to see them do well in all things they do."

"You sure? It's clear that you weren't supportive of their success as a teacher, purposely holding back certain players from playing in the playoffs."

"That's not fair and you know it," Wanda said as her friendly smiled turned into a cold scowl. "I don't fail students because I want them to fail. I fail them so they can work to improve themselves. You know I care about my students, every single one of them, like they were my own children."

"Do you even know anything about football? Won't you just feel lost the whole time?"

Wanda now knew what he was doing. He wanted to push her buttons and see how far he would have to go to get under her skin. He wanted her to doubt herself, to doubt her ability. It wouldn't work. She was going to stand her ground like she did every time with Coach, never getting angry. "I don't, but I was hoping you could teach me a bit about it."

Coach, a bit surprised, agreed to help her learn. Wanda made her way to the seat closest to the screen and sat down, her keys clanking against the metal frame of the desk and chair. Wanda listened carefully as Coach talked about interceptions, penalties, positions, and scoring. Being a former basketball coach, she connected various aspects of the game to basketball, gradually enhancing her understanding. This is what she wanted. She wanted to gain the trust of those whose she had not gained yet.

As the day neared its end and Wanda sunk into her chair, she cried. Why was she crying? She didn't know. All she knew was that crying felt like the right thing to do at the moment. It had been a long and stressful day, trying to learn the ins and outs of her new job. Her mind wandered back to Michelle. She wondered what Michelle was doing right now. Was she playing in the garden with George? Was she eating a snack? Was she napping? Was she waiting for her mother to get home? She didn't know exactly what she was doing, but she knew she missed her daughter.

As Wanda picked up a tissue to wipe her eyes, there was a soft knock at the door. Wanda looked up to see her administrative assistant, Allison Schmidt. Allison was a tall and slender woman, a few years younger than Wanda, with flowing brown hair that reminded everyone of a shimmering brown eye in the sunset. She and Wanda knew each other from brief encounters, but nothing more.

"Are you okay Mrs. Hare?" Allison asked as she propped her tall and slender body up against the doorframe.

"Please," Wanda sniffled. "Call me Wanda. I'm okay, today has just been a lot." Wanda looked down at the tissue and saw streaks of black mascara littering the paper. Embarrassed, she began wiping her eyes again to get the rest of the smeared mascara off.

"Wanda," Allison said with a smile. "I like that. You're going to be a different principal, aren't you? One with true principles to match."

Wanda smiled. "That's my goal, anyway. I want the staff and faculty to know I'm approachable, and that I will always have their backs against all odds. I want to show the students the care and respect I gave them as a teacher."

"Well, I know it's only your first day, but so far you're doing a mighty fine job, Ma'am."

"Allison, thank you for that. I really appreciate your support. I'm going to be leaning on you a lot this year while I learn the ins and outs of the job."

"And that is exactly what I am here for," Allison said as she bumbled through her purse.

Wanda, still trying to scrub the streaky mascara off, replied, "Allison, are you married? Do you have kids?"

Allison pulled her hand out of her purse and extended her hand to Wanda, revealing a pack of makeup wipes to help her clean up her mascara. "Yes Ma'am, I have a husband of ten years and three kids - a son and two daughters."

"I've been married for thirteen years now. I have a daughter, Michelle, who means the world to me. You know, she's the reason I took this job. I was afraid of the backlash I might face being a female principal, not only from the students, but from some of the faculty as well. It terrified me because I saw the torment and hatred that Shawn Carlile went through when he first made his way into administration. I was also afraid of the backlash my daughter may face from some kids in her grade. Kids can be cruel, and they parrot what their parents say often. But ultimately, I did it to show her that anything was possible for her. That, just because she was a woman, she could be whatever she wanted to be."

"Lordy Wanda," Allison said as she sleeved away at the tears gently sliding down her cheeks. "Bringing tears to my eyes. You're not only an inspiration to your daughter, but to all the women who work in the school system. When I heard you were going to be our new Principal, I was so excited. It's a significant moment for us to break down those barriers! You're a trailblazer."

"Sadly, it's not been easy."

"What do you mean? Wasn't today your first day?" Allison quirked an eyebrow as she looked at Wanda.

"Yes, but I had one member of the school already buck up against me. I'm not going to say their name, but they were very adamant that I was not meant for this job. It was hard to stay composed while I was being degraded. But I did it. I did it for Michelle." Wanda confessed.

"You're the Principal now!" Allison snapped. "Why would one of your employees be so nasty towards you?"

"Sadly, it's the world we live in right now, Allison."

Michelle sat crisscrossed at the large window in their sunroom, patiently waiting for her mother to come home. She was an expert on what time school ended, because of her counting down the hours when she was actually in school, so she was becoming worried. School got out at 3:00 pm, but it was almost 6:00 pm and she still didn't see her mother.

Michelle ran to her dad, who was dozing off in his recliner, and jumped in his lap. Jolting up from his half slumber to the sudden impact of Michelle landing on his lap, he looked at her and said, "'Chlle, s'evrything okay?"

"No, Daddy!" she exclaimed worriedly. "Mommy isn't home yet. I know what time school gets out and she should be home by now!"

George chuckled, causing Michelle to look at him with a frustrated look. *"Why isn't he more worried about Mommy! She could be in trouble."* She thought to herself.

"Baby, yer Mama will be home sho'tly. Just 'cause school ends at three don't mean she gets off at three. Yer Mama works 'till five."

"Oh…" Michelle started. Before she could continue her sentence, she saw a set of headlights rounding the dusty road that led to the house. She jumped off her dad's lap and rushed to the window. With her nose pressed against the glass, her hands supporting her body against the window, a smile crept across her face as she saw her mother's 1970's sky blue Mustang come around the corner.

Michelle ran swiftly out of the house to where her mother parked her car. As the door opened, Michelle found her way to her mother's lap where she buried her head and exclaimed, "I missed you, Mommy!"

"Oh Sweetie, I missed you too!" Wanda said, slowly standing up with her daughter attached. As she wiggled her daughter from between her legs, she leaned into the car to get the rest of her stuff. She grabbed her purse, her jacket, and her briefcase. While making sure everything was in order, she found a pack of makeup wipes in her purse. With a smile, she remembered her conversation with Allison and the amazing support she received.

"Mommy, come on!" Michelle said as she tugged at Wanda's pants.

"I'm coming sweetie, I'm coming," Wanda laughed as she followed her daughter inside.

"How was your day, Mommy?" Michelle asked as they both crossed the threshold of the house.

"It was good, Honey. Let me tell you about my chair. I think you would really like it. It's taller than you! And it's fluffy like a puppy, you just sink into it like a cloud," Wanda said as she got down on her knees to be eye level with Michelle. "But most importantly," she paused.

"Uh-huh!"

"It spins in circles and goes *really* fast!" Wanda finished as she leaned in to kiss Michelle's forehead. Michelle smiled and kissed her mother back on her head.

"Now how's your day gone?" George asked as he and Wanda closed the door to Michelle's room. "You been off all nigh'."

"George," she said, stopping him at the top of the staircase and leaning her head against his chest. "It was okay."

George wrapped his arm around his wife, pulling her closer, and leading her down the stairs. "Hunny, lemme tell you somethin'. Jus' okay isn't good 'nough for me. Tell me what happened," George said as they reached the bottom step.

"I love you so much," she said, as she followed behind him to the living room. "It wasn't bad. Robert, you remember him, right? Sure, you do. So, he came by and talked to me for a bit. I feel like he's really gonna support me."

"Tha's good Hunny. What els' happened?"

"Well, I ran into the football coach. He was rude and accused me of not being good enough for the job. It was really what I was afraid of. He did, however, teach me about football. I know that if the ball gets to the end zone, that team gets six points!"

"Tha's good Hunny. Real good."

"Do you remember Willie's youngest daughter, Allison? Allison Schmidt?" Wanda asked. "She's married to Harry."

"Yessum, I do. Real sweet lady."

"Yes, she is! She made me feel great. She told me I was an inspiration to other women."

"Tha's good Hunny," George said, kissing his wife's head. "You ready fo' the firs' day of school for the kids?"

"Oh, we never are!" Wanda laughed as she made her way, sleepily, to her bed and looked over at the local news on the TV. On the screen the newscaster said, **"Coming Up Next: Holcomb County's First Female Principal."** Wanda smiled and looked over at the confused look on George's face. "Oh yeah, that happened," she smiled.

"Yer famous Hunny! Tha's an important detail to have left ou'. I'm so prouda ya, Wanda." George smiled.

Wanda crawled into bed and closed her eyes as she listened to the TV quietly tell her story. She couldn't help but to think about what Allison had told her, *"'You're not only an inspiration to your daughter, but to all the women who work in the school system.'"* It made Wanda feel good. It made her finally feel like the decision to accept the position - the decision that made her toss and turn at night for the last few weeks - was the right decision. Not only for Michelle, but for all the other women out there.

Chapter 3
The Other First Day

After the rollercoaster of emotions Wanda's first day invoked, she felt sure she was ready for the official first day of school. All the students, faculty, and staff would be on the school grounds for the first time under her careful watch. Despite the negatives that came along with her official first day, she had hoped that her next first day would go smoothly. As she sat up in her bed, finding the covers still turned down from when George got up at dawn to tend to the garden, she rubbed the fuzzies out of her eyes. Wanda made her way into the kitchen to begin her breakfast. Her tradition of pancakes and bacon on the first day of school was one she'd started on her first day as a teacher.

She vividly remembered her first day teaching. School started on a Friday that year, just like this year. The students were restless and couldn't wait for the weekend. Her goal was to create a comfortable learning environment for her students on their first day back at school. Her first class, however, was not the best class to have. Many of the students had been held back from the previous year, several of them were repeat offenders, and very few wanted to learn. It was a challenge getting them all interested on the first day, but it was something she obtained.

Wanda was a very animated teacher, who spoke in fluid actions and crisp words, giving each character of the books a distinct voice when she read aloud. She wanted to encourage the students to use their imagination to make the books she taught enjoyable, making it into a mental movie of their own. She remembered when the students first came into the classroom, the noise of their voices drowning out the sound of the bell as the lever clanged against it. As Wanda tried to corral the kids and get them to pay attention, they got louder and louder. Her idea, her very first idea as a teacher, was to climb on her desk and perform a scene from *Hamlet*. She began, in a unique voice:

"To be, or not to be, that is the question: Whether 'tis nobler in the mind to suffer the slings and arrows of outrageous fortune, or to take arms against a sea of troubles and by opposing end them. To die—to sleep, no more; and by a sleep to say we end the heart-ache and the thousand natural shocks that flesh is heir to: 'tis a consummation devoutly to be wish'd. To die, to sleep; to sleep, perchance to dream—ay, there's the rub: For in that sleep of death what dreams may come, when we have shuffled off this mortal coil, must give us pause—there's the respect that makes calamity of so long life."

By the end of her performance, the class had quieted down and were staring at Wanda - whether in awe of her performance or shocked that she had done it. As *"... there's the respect that makes calamity of so long life."* escaped her lips, the entire class burst into applause, many standing up as they did. It made Wanda feel appreciated and respected, but most importantly it gave her confidence that she would be just fine. A confidence that she had carried with her ever since.

Her hands wrapped warmly around her coffee mug; her memory ended. She could smell the bacon frying on the stove, the smell of the open syrup bottle filled her nose, and the warmth of her coffee warmed her body. Confidence radiated from her. She was confident that everything would be alright.

Wanda pulled into the school parking lot, only to be met with a set of blue police lights parked by one of the school buses. As she parked, she quickly hopped out of her Mustang and scurried over to where the action was. The school's Safety Resource Officer, Deputy Cooke, was standing outside the accordion doors of the bus, speaking with a student. As Wanda got closer, she could see drips of blood rolling from the student's nose. *"A fight on the first day?"* she thought to herself.

"Principal Hare," Deputy Cooke said, turning to see Wanda making her way to him.

"Please, call me Wanda. What is going on here?"

"Well Wanda, this student and another got into a fight when the bus pulled onto the school grounds. Apparently, it was over a girl that neither boy really liked, and it escalated out of control."

"I'll take them from here," she said as she turned to the student standing next to him. Upon further examination, Wanda recognized the junior beside Deputy Cooke. "Sam, over a girl?" she asked, with a disapproving tone dragging behind it.

"I'm sorry ma'am. I just couldn't take his mouth anymore," Sam started.

"Nah man, this motherfucker swung at me first," the other student shouted from out the bus window, where he had been listening from the whole time. Wanda recognized this student as well. Craig Jennings, a senior, was one of the school's star football players.

"Enough." Wanda stated, almost demanding their attention. "We will settle this in my office. Let's go, both of you." The students chased Wanda, one on each side of her, to separate them from one another.

As they approached her office, Allison looked at the two boys coming in beside Wanda and smiled, "Welcome to your first school day, Ma'am." Wanda, holding back a laugh, smiled at Allison as she went by and entered her office. The smile quickly faded as she closed the door behind her and looked at the two boys, who had now slumped into the chairs facing her desk. "I'm extremely disappointed right now, gentlemen," she said as she walked around her desk to her chair. "I know you are both capable of being better than this. Sam, you are one of the brightest students in this school. Craig, you are the star running back for our football team. Are you both just willing to throw away those things over a girl? A girl who neither of you likes?"

The boys sat in silence; their faces almost buried in the ground because of their embarrassment. Wanda sat silently, letting the boys collect their thoughts and giving them time to process what she had said. After a few minutes, Craig looked up and said, "Mrs. Hare, I'm sorry I cussed at you earlier. I lost my cool." He turned his head to look at Sam and continued, "Sam, man, I'm really sorry I freaked out on you. I was frustrated with Erica, and I took it out on you."

Sam looked back at Craig and said, "Man, I don't care about Erica. What happened, happened. It escalated and it should not have gotten to that point. I'm sorry for punching you first."

Sam reached his hand out towards Craig, the two boys gripping each other's hand tightly. "Thank you, boys, that's all I wanted," Wanda began before her door slung open, slamming against the wall and rattling Wanda's desk. Through the door followed Coach's short but stout frame. Wanda jumped out of her seat, her hands pressed firmly on her desk, and calmly said, "Coach, what is the meaning of this?"

"I knew you would do it. I just knew you would do it. You got one of my best damn players in here and you're going to ruin the beginning of his season. Over what? A little spat?" Coach shouted as he looked at the two boys. "And with this one? It surely couldn't have been much of a fight!" he finished, pointing at Sam with ferocity in his voice.

"Coach," Craig began.

"I'll deal with you later. Now get out of here!" Coach screamed. Coach had been so loud that Deputy Cooke came into the room to make sure everything was okay.

"Boys, you're dismissed. Deputy Cooke, everything is fine here. Would you mind closing the door on your way out?" She asked as she waited for everyone but Coach to leave the room. After the latch in the door clicked into its hole, Wanda continued, "Coach, I will not tolerate this kind of behavior under my administration. I understand that past administrations may have allowed you to act out like this, but I will not. We should not expose these students to this attitude. They look to you as a role model and you blatantly disrespect me in front of them? How dare you treat me like that in front of students, sir! You can talk to me any way you would like in private, but in front of students, I will not accept this kind of behavior."

"No, you listen to me," Coach started.

"No, Coach. This isn't a negotiation. I said what I said, and I meant it. Next time you have an outburst like this in front of students, you will receive a written warning. This is your verbal one."

"Oh, you have got to be shitting me," he said as he rolled his eyes into the back of his head.

"Coach. Enough," Wanda said, still as cool as she had been in the beginning, as she sat back down in her chair and leaned back. She crossed her left leg across her right knee and pulled her hands together. "Now, is there anything else I can do for you, Coach?"

"No," he responded coldly. He turned away from looking at Wanda and made his way to the door with his tail between his legs.

"Coach," Wanda called, stopping him in his tracks. "Craig wasn't going to be in trouble. I wanted to talk to them, not punish them. It's the first day. Cut him some slack. I did."

Coach, without saying a word, looked down at his feet like a scorned dog. He made his way through the door.

Moving out of Coach's way as he made his way out of the office, Allison snuck into Wanda's office and looked at her with excitement in her eyes. "Wanda, that was simply amazing. I couldn't help but to hear the conversation, and the way you handled Coach? Wow! I have never seen someone talk to Coach like that, but I also haven't ever seen that look of dismay in his eyes."

"Thank you, Allison," she began, before pausing and looking into the distance. "It felt good to get those boys to understand what they did wrong and to apologize to one another without me having to tell them to. I really feel like I made a breakthrough with those two just from one conversation. I wanted to reinforce the students, let them know how valuable they are, and I really did it," she said, turning her attention back to Allison. Despite the

"Good morning, Panthers!" Wanda said, with genuine excitement in her voice, to the microphone. She could hear the echo of her voice ringing throughout the hallways. It was her first homeroom announcement as Principal. "This is your new Principal, Mrs. Wanda Hare. I hope you all had a wonderful summer vacation, and I'm glad you're all back with us today. Now, I know it is a Friday, but let's get through the day so we can enjoy our weekend!" Wanda paused as she read the lunch menu to herself.

"For lunch today, we will have chicken tenders, mashed potatoes, a roll, and for dessert, sponge cake," she continued. "One more thing before we start the day, students. I am proud of each and every one of you, what you have accomplished, and what you will accomplish. My door is always open, whenever you need me." She finished as the bell for first period rang over the PA system.

Wanda sat back in her chair as she listened to the many voices of boys and girls; African American, Caucasian, Hispanic, Asian, and purple; athletes and academia, all mixing into one cacophony. The sound brought a smile to her face, a sound of diversity and the beginning of her first school year as Principal.

As lunch approached, Wanda made her way to the lunchroom. She had decided to be a lunch monitor all day to meet the students she didn't know and greet the ones she knew. With her radio hooked to her lift pants pocket and her keys dangling from her right belt loop, she made her way down the halls.

Reaching the quiet hollowness of the cafeteria, she made her way to the back to greet her lunch staff. At the register was Wayne, the youngest member of the entire school staff. He was a ripe 25 years old. He was an astute young man who had come across some hardships in life, causing him to pause his dreams and take the first job he could get. Despite facing hardships in life, he maintained a powerful motivation and consistently put in 100% effort.

Next, she saw the lunch lady who worked the line, Minnie. Minnie was a beautiful African American woman in her mid-forties. She worked the line and loved the students. She was always bubbly, cheery, and kind. Her soulful eyes spoke to the students and made them feel like she was family. She enjoyed nothing more than being around the students, listening to their stories, and mothering them.

As she crossed into the kitchen, she saw the Head Cook, Caroline. Caroline and Wanda's mother had been friends for a long time. Wanda knew Caroline's cooking skills were top-notch. She could have easily been working at a fancy restaurant for more money. She wanted to be here, though. Despite being offered multiple positions at those fancier restaurants, she kept refusing. Once, Wanda asked her what made her so attached to the school and Caroline simply responded, *"The students. I want to make sure every student has the opportunity to eat at least one good meal a day."*

"Hello Caroline!" she smiled as she walked to the prep table Caroline was working on.

"Hello Mrs. Hare!" She happily replied, laying her knife down next to the sheet pan filled with cake.

"Please Sweetie, it's Wanda. This looks fantastic. Mind if I try a piece?" Wanda asked, pointing at the sponge cake sitting on the table beside her.

"Oh, absolutely Honey," she said as she cut a square piece of cake out and handed it to Wanda on a white paper plate with a matching plastic fork.

Wanda took one bite of the sponge cake and her eyes lit up. "Is this Momma's recipe?"

"Yes, ma'am it sure is. Your Momma gave it to me over the summer. How does it taste compared to hers?"

"It's delicious, Caroline! It tastes just like Momma's, moist and sweet. The kids are going to love it!" she said, right before the bell rang again, signaling the beginning of the first lunch. Wanda said her goodbyes to the kitchen staff as she made her way to the front of the lunchroom. As the students swarmed in like a pack of hungry hyenas, Wanda repeated a line of 'Hello's and 'Good to see you's.' Her smile was permanently painted on her face as the students came in, making them feel welcomed and at home.

Wanda looked over as she heard a girl shouting across the cafeteria, "Mrs. Hare! Mrs. Hare!" throwing her hand up occasionally, almost to let Wanda know where she was like a game of Marco Polo. As the voice, and hand, got closer, Wanda recognized the student. Katherine Church was a very intelligent senior, with flowing blonde hair that radiated in the light like a sparkling star in the moonlight. Katherine was an eccentric character, bubbly and outgoing. She was an active women's rights advocate and promoted it every chance she received.

"Well hello Katherine," Wanda said as Katherine made her way past the last student in between them. "How are you today?"

"Oh, I am great!" she said with a sparkle in her eyes. "When I heard over the summer that you were going to be our new Principal, I was ecstatic! Finally, a woman is in charge. You flexed your girl muscles and came out on top, Mrs. Hare!"

"Well, thank you Katherine," Wanda said humbly. "I didn't flex any muscles. They offered me the position. Applying for it never crossed my mind, but they wanted me for the job."

"Of course, they did! You're a superstar of a woman. The way you taught Robert Frost," Katherine said as she twirled around. "*'Two roads diverged in a wood, and I—I took the one less traveled by, and that has made all the difference.'* That's you Mrs. Hare! You took the road less traveled and that was the difference! You are the first female principal - first female administrator - in all of Holcomb County! Just, wow!" she said, as she reached out to grab Wanda's hand and shake it.

"Thank you, Katherine, that's sweet of you to say. I just want to be the best principal I can, one that students know they can come to, and they trust. I hope I can do that to make you even more proud."

"Oh, you already have made me extremely proud! I heard about what happened with Coach today, and wow!"

"Wait, what?" Wanda's smile faded. "What did you hear exactly?"

"Well, I heard Coach came in there yelling and throwing his hands around," she said as she mimicked the motions she described. "Then you calmly told Craig and Sam to leave. Then you closed the door! By the time he came out, he looked like a woman had scorned him! It was amazing! Like, wow! How did you have the courage to stand up to Coach? He's frightening."

"Where did you hear this from, Ms. Church?" Wanda asked with a bit of an irritated tone seeping out of her voice. "That was a private happening this morning."

"Well, I heard it from Becky, who heard it from Steve, who heard it from Earl, who heard it from..."

"It's fine, Katherine," Wanda said before Katherine rattled off the entire student body. Coach and I did have a discussion this morning, that's the truth. It was not as violent or harsh as everybody's making it out to be. A simple misunderstanding, really. Remember, don't listen to every rumor you hear. I'm sure over the next couple of months what you hear about me won't be 100% accurate. I'm sure they will say some derogatory things about me and some nasty rumors will swirl, but don't listen to them. Come to me and talk to me first."

"Yes, Ma'am!" Katherine gleaned. "Well, I'm going to eat before all the good food is gone!"

"Katherine!" Wanda called as Katherine walked toward the lunch line. "Ask for two slices of the sponge cake," she said as she winked at the girl and smiled.

As the day wound down, Wanda heard the screeching of the last bell of the day, followed by the insurmountable sound of the diverse student body. She looked up from the forms she had filled out and looked at the clock. *"Three o'clock already? Well, today sure flew by."*

Wanda heard a knock at the door revealing Craig standing there with his book bag hanging from one arm and his gym bag from the other. "Principal Hare, do you have a minute?"

"Certainly Craig, come on in and sit," she said as she sat her pen down and shuffled the forms into a tray on her desk. "What can I do for you?"

"I want to apologize."

With a soft smile penciled across her thin lips, Wanda said, "You already did that, and all is forgiven. I just want to make sure you realize how special you are and encourage you to not throw out your future over little things like girls."

"Thank you, Principal Hare, but not for that. I want to apologize, on behalf of most of the football team, for the way Coach acted today," Craig corrected. Wanda blinked rapidly a few times before leaning back in her chair. Craig continued, "It really disappointed me with how he handled it, and it bothered me all day. I told a couple of the guys and they agreed with me."

"Craig," Wanda said, holding back a tear. "Thank you. I know every student in this school can achieve so much, and I just want to make sure they are enabled at school.

You don't need to apologize for Coach's actions, but I appreciate it."

"I want you to know, also, that you have the respect of the football team's players." He smiled and stood. "I have to get to practice now, but I just wanted to say that and thank you for this morning. See you tomorrow, Ma'am." As Craig turned to head to practice, he came face-to-face with Robert.

"Craig, running late to practice?" Robert said as he put his hands out to stop the boy from colliding with him.

"Yes Sir," Craig said, looking down at his feet.

"Let's get you a note, son, so you don't have to worry about an extra hard practice. Go see Mrs. Schmidt and she'll take care of you." As Craig said his goodbyes and thank you, Robert turned back to Wanda. "How was your first day, Ma'am?"

"It was good. I really enjoyed it, actually. Well, except the part when Mr. Caves room had a fire," she joked.

"On fire? I didn't hear about that one! Please tell me more," he laughed.

"Well, you know how Caves is really eccentric and out there," Wanda laughed as she began the story.

"Much like a certain former English teacher I know..." Robert winked at her.

Wanda smiled with a slight chuckle. "Well, he comes to school today, dressed as a wizard, for God knows why. Then, in his third period Environmental Science class, he was dropping pumice rocks in water to show

how they floated. Well, he dropped one in one of the student's water bottles and it sank. Mind-boggling for Caves, so he grabs the bottle and brings it to the front of the room, pours it into a beaker and lights a match. Up in flames it went."

"What in the world?"

"Then I had to suspend a student for bringing alcohol on school grounds," she finished.

"Wow," Robert laughed again. "What a first day."

"It's just one thing that makes me love this job already. Never a dull moment," Wanda smiled. She perked up and said, "Remember Katherine Church?"

"Uh, vaguely," Robert said as he scratched his head. "Blonde hair? Twelfth grade?"

"Yes sir, that's her," she confirmed. "I think I'm going to offer her a work study position for her instead of an elective this semester. She seemed amazed that I was the principal and I think having her work beside me may do her some good. Really get her on track."

"That's a great idea Wanda," Robert said as he paused for a minute and glanced around the room. As his attention made it back to Wanda, he finished, "Are you going to tell me what happened with Coach this morning?"

"Robert, I really don't want to talk about it to be honest. It happened and it's over."

"Wanda, he has no right to talk to you like that," Robert scoffed.

"Robert, it's fine. I don't think it will happen again anytime soon. I still don't understand how word got out so quickly about what happened." Wanda sighed and slowed her eyes as she remembered her prior run-in with Coach.

"Kids will be kids, Ma'am," Robert chuckled. "I want you to remember I support whatever decisions you make. Just let me know what you need from me. I'm glad you had a good *other* first day."

"Thank you, Robert, I truly appreciate your support."

As Robert made his way out of Wanda's office, he turned around to see Allison holding her purse, patiently waiting her turn to talk to Wanda. The pair slid past each other, Robert leaving and Allison entering.

"Hello Wanda!" Allison said, with her signature smile painted across her lips. "Are you okay if I head out, Ma'am?"

"Of course, Allison. Thank you for your hard work today," Wanda replied while an innocent and sweet smile crept across her face. "But I have one question for you," she requested. Allison and she had become very close over the last two weeks, and she valued her opinion. "How did I do today?"

"Fantastic." Allison was beaming. She was so impressed with Wanda and loved that she cared about her feedback. "I had several students, staff, and faculty compliment you today. They all talked about how they felt you listened and cared, that you wanted to make a difference in this school. And I think they're right."

"Thank you, Allison. You have a wonderful weekend and I'll see you next week." Wanda sat back in her chair as Allison left. She smiled and thought to herself, *"I really did it."*

Chapter 4
Friday Night Lights

T he day was winding down as Wanda watched the clock on her wall tick to 3:00. Dealing with teacher disputes and troubled students made for a full day, but she was still excited about the first football game of the season. It was also their homecoming game, so Wanda would be there to rile up the crowd during half-time.

She loved going to the games, even as a teacher, because she knew so many of the students. To see them transform from their everyday selves into gritty and determined football players was wonderful. She had taught many of the students playing and loved supporting them. She also wanted to see Craig play. He had become one of the first students she'd become close with after the incident on the first day of school.

A knock at the door revealed the very student she had just been thinking about, Craig. He was dressed in the navy blue and grey jersey of the East Holcomb Panthers, his black hair slicked back, and a gym bag dangling from his side. He was bright eyed and ready for the game tonight. "Hi Mrs. Hare," he proudly said.

"Craig!" she called back. "To what do I owe the pleasure?"

"I just wanted to stop by and see if you were going to the game tonight," he said with hope blatantly in his voice. "I sure would love to have you there."

"Of course, I'll be there!" Wanda smiled. "I wouldn't miss the Panthers' first home game. How are you feeling about it?"

"I'm really excited," Craig said with a smile across his face. "This game should be an easy win for us to start off the season. It'll be an even sweeter win knowing we got the W from North Holcomb, too," he said, smiling proudly. Craig was surrounded by an aura of confidence. His confidence wasn't an unnerving cockiness, but more of an assurance in himself and his abilities. Craig was also a smart student who got straight-A's and worked hard in both his classes and on the field. What

Wanda respected most about him, however, was the respect he held towards others. His apology on behalf of the football team had earned her respect and admiration.

"I'm excited to do that, Craig! So, how many yards do you plan to rush for tonight? One hundred?"

"I'm shooting for one fifty," he replied, almost matter-of-factly. As Craig finished his sentence, the familiar call of his name rang from the lobby. It was Coach.

"Craig! Field! Now!" Coach called as he made his way towards Wanda's office and slid past Craig. "Prince, how you doin' today?"

"I'm fine Coach. How about yourself?" Since their conversation on the first day of school, standing up to him, Wanda had commanded a new air of respect from Coach. It may have been from the embarrassment of the entire school knowing what happened between the two or the threat of receiving a write-up, but either way, she was glad that things had become much more civil between the two.

"I'm doin' good. I'm excited about the first game tonight. Our Panthers are ready to whoop some Rattlesnake ASS!" He excitedly yelled. Catching Wanda's disapproving look, he corrected "Sorry. Tail."

Wanda smiled. "Coach, I know we have had our differences, but the thing I have always respected most about you is your dedication and passion for the team.

I just want you to know you have my full support in the future regarding the team."

Coach, obviously stunned, responded, "Thank you, Ma'am." It was the first time he had ever called Wanda something other than 'Prince'. She could tell that, even though he didn't outright say it, respect was now mutual. "Are you still going to give a hype speech during half-time? I know our guys are really looking forward to it."

"Oh, absolutely Coach, I'll be sure to get the crowd and the players fired up!" She smiled.

At five o'clock, Wanda made her way to the football field. It was an especially chilly day, so she sported her favorite grey and black Panthers jacket. The game started at 6:00 pm, so she wanted to get there a little early to interact with the students and parents. That was one of her favorite things about going to the games. She loved seeing all the students dressed in grey or navy blue, supporting their team, and full of school spirit. Her goal was to achieve a new student turnout record for today's game. She had been busy firing up the students and the team with Spirit Week and pep rallies this past week.

As she approached the field, she could see the opposing team's travel bus parked in the full parking lot for the field. She was an hour early and the parking lot was already full. Surely her hope was going to be met with reality. She smiled as she saw the sea of navy blue and grey flooding in through the gates. Some wore school shirts, others had mini pompoms, and most had painted faces. School spirit was alive and well, something she had made a year-long goal to accomplish.

Making her way across the crowded parking lot, she heard her name being called from behind her. "Mrs. Hare! Mrs. Hare! Wait for me!" the voice called. As Wanda turned around, she saw Katherine running towards her, waving a pad in her hand and sporting a pen behind her ear.

"Hello Katherine," Wanda called back as she turned around and came to a halt to wait for her. Wanda had offered Katherine a work study position in her office, and she was set to start in the next week, but she looked like she was ready to start tonight.

"Thank... you..." Katherine said, out of breath, as she arrived where Wanda was standing. "I'm glad I saw you. I was really hoping to run into you. Would it be possible for me to shadow you tonight, just kind of observe what you do?"

"Is that what the pad and pen are for?"

"Oh, this?" she said as she held the notepad up to Wanda's face. "No, this is for the school newspaper. The student who was supposed to cover the game got sick, so I offered to take the story! Mainly so that I could observe you, if I'm being honest with you."

Wanda wasn't sure if she should take this as a compliment or be worried. She knew Katherine had good intentions, but she came off strong with her words and actions. It was borderline stalker-ish. Wanda brushed these thoughts away and responded, "Sure you can, Sweetie, I'd love to have you keep me company for the game."

With that, Katherine began jumping up and down, clapping her hands together between the notepad and pen. "Thank you, thank you, thank you!" she exclaimed. Wanda motioned for her to follow as she turned back around and made her way towards the gate.

As Wanda approached the line to the gate, someone interrupted her again. This time, though, Deputy Cooke met her. "Wanda let's skip this line and get you in through the side gate," he said as he approached her. Noticing that Katherine had been trailing her, he glanced over and smiled. "You too, young lady."

Before Wanda could protest, he spoke up again. "I don't want to hear an argument, Ma'am," he laughed. "Aside from the game, you're the star of the attraction."

Rather than engage in a losing argument, she went with Deputy Cooke and Katherine to the side gate. She didn't want special treatment; she would much rather wait in line with the rest of the crowd. Knowing that things like this would happen more often now that she was Principal didn't make her like it any more.

Finally, to the side gate, Deputy Cooke unlocked the gate and opened it, allowing Wanda and Katherine to make their way into the game without waiting. Katherine was following closely behind Wanda when she looked around at the excitement of the upcoming football game. Wanda glanced behind her and noticed that Katherine seemed mesmerized and in awe of the surroundings. "Have you ever been to a football game, Katherine?" Wanda asked.

"Well, this is kind of embarrassing, but no. I've never been into sports like that and had no desire to come to a game. But. I see now that this is much more than a sporting event. This is about school spirit. Rivalries. There's so much laughter and joy in here, it's refreshing."

Wanda knew exactly what she meant. The excitement that radiated through the air, the sound of the music blaring through the PA system playing songs like "Living on a Prayer" and "Nothing's Gonna Stop Us Now", the way the lights lit up the navy-blue Panthers carefully painted across the middle of the field, the smell of popcorn and hot dogs filling your nose, it was more exciting than the carnival. "You're right Katherine, it *is* more than a football game," Wanda said with a smile.

As halftime quickly approached, Wanda watched the Panthers outscore their opponents, 28-3. Wanda was happy that she understood what was happening in the game after her learning session with Coach on her very first day. She taught Katherine the rules of the game so that she could follow along as well.

Craig led the offensive assault, racking up 175 yards in the first half. Wanda was happy to see Craig exceeding his own expectations - and hers, for that matter.

Katherine returned to her seat beside Wanda with two large bags of popcorn and two diet sodas. "Here you are, Ma'am!"

"Well, thank you, Katherine," Wanda said, as she took the bag of popcorn. "You certainly didn't have to do that."

"Well, you didn't have to let me shadow you today or teach me about football, but you did! I've learned a lot from you, Mrs. Hare. Not only about football, but about how to carry yourself, how to give and earn respect from people. Just watching you go around, talking to student after student, parents, teachers, everyone that you could. School spirit is so high tonight!"

Wanda hadn't thought about how many more people were here supporting the home team than there had been in the past. As she looked around the stadium, she couldn't find an empty seat in the stands, something that had never happened since she began teaching there. *"Surely it isn't because of me, we just always seem to have a better turnout year after year,"* she thought to herself.

As if she could read Wanda's mind, Katherine chirped, "And it's thanks to you! Honestly. I've heard many people say that you make them happy to go here, proud to go here! The way you speak to the students and really, truly listen to us garners a lot of respect from the students. They love the new culture you have created for the school."

"Thank you, Katherine. That means a lot," Wanda said, holding in a tear from slowly falling down her cheek. She leaned in closer to Katherine and continued, "Sometimes, I doubt myself. I question if I'm doing the right thing here. All I want to do is to be the best I can be for the students, to help them learn in a positive and engaging environment, to allow them to be proud of being a Panther. Otherwise, I'm failing my students."

Katherine looked over at Wanda as a solitary tear sliding down her cheek glistened in the bright stadium lights. "Are you okay?"

"Yes Katherine, just have something in my eye," Wanda lied, as she reached up and wiped away her tear. As the clock turned down to zero, Wanda stood up to make her way down to the field to give her halftime speech. Katherine stood, preparing to follow her down to the field. "Katherine, I'm afraid they won't allow you on the field with me during my speech."

"I had a feeling that would happen," Katherine said, a hint of disappointment in her voice. She sat back down, almost pouting.

Wanda looked back over at her, smiling, and said, "Plus, you need to be closer to the speakers so you can write what I'm saying for your article."

Katherine perked up. She had almost forgotten the whole reason she was there. She had taken a couple of notes, mainly things Wanda relayed to her about the inner workings of the game. This would be the highlight of her piece, though. "Sounds good to me!"

Her feet crunching spilled popcorn, and avoiding spilled soda, Wanda walked back down the bleachers, feeling the vibrations with every step. As she reached the gravel at the end of the bleachers, she felt a nervous sensation set in.

She wasn't sure if she was ready to give this speech, she was afraid she would forget what to say. Speaking in front of hundreds of students was easy for her, but this was in front of thousands of people, including parents, teachers, and the press. If she had to guess, there were probably over 1,700 people in attendance, filling the seats and the fence line around the field!

She took a deep breath and continued to the field where she was to give her speech. The dance team was ending their routine as Wanda opened the gate to get on the field. As she made her way to the middle of the field, she smiled as the dancers came by, telling them they did a phenomenal job in their performance. She took the microphone from the AV club student and eagerly listened for the announcement that she would deliver a speech.

As the music slowly died down, she felt her hands sweat and her heart rate increase. Her nerves were setting in. She closed her eyes and took a deep breath, pushing the feelings and thoughts of nervousness out of her mind. The announcement came from the press box, "Ladies and gentlemen, may I have your attention please!" the voice called out, as the voices in the stadium died down. "If you will redirect your attention to the center of the field. Mrs. Hare, our East Holcomb Principal, would like to share a few words with you."

As the echo of the announcer quietly echoed away off the metal bleachers, Wanda took one final deep breath and opened her eyes. "Ladies and Gentlemen! Students, parents, staff and faculty, members of the community, thank you all for being here tonight," she began.

"How's everyone doing tonight?" She yelled as the crowd erupted in joyous applause and shouts. It was at that moment that Wanda knew she was going to be okay. "How about those Panthers! Here we are. Ready to write a new script for East Holcomb. Ready to tackle the change and create new memories, new inspirations, new records.

"Throughout the County, East Holcomb has come to be known as a classy, dedicated, and tough school, full of athletes and intellectuals. Full of dreamers and doers. Full of friends and family. All the students in attendance tonight, please stand up," she paused as a wave of students stood up across the stadium. "These are the students who have built the East Holcomb culture! These are the students who have made East Holcomb full of hope and happiness," she paused as the crowd erupted in applause.

"Tonight. Tonight, we're here to watch our Panthers play against our cross-town rivals," she said, facing the football players coming out of the locker room. "You are the heroes tonight. You are the ones who are fighting, taking the hits, making the plays, to make these people excited. The buzz you have created in this stadium tonight is amazing. But it's not just about the eleven young men taking the field - this school is a family!

"It has truly been an honor over the last several weeks to get to know many of you, to learn your names, and to learn your heart and grit," she said, turning back to the audience. "Finally, I urge all of you, players and students alike, to enjoy your life, the precious moments you have. We. Are. The Panthers!" she finished as the whole stadium stood up and erupted in applause that could be heard across the county.

As Wanda handed the microphone back to the AV student, she noticed Coach walking towards her, still clapping. Following his lead, the players stood up and began towards the middle of the field. Coach reached out his hand to Wanda when he arrived, gripping her hand tightly and whispering a quiet thank you.

"Boys! Let's give it up for Mrs. Hare!" Coach shouted, taking the microphone from the AV student. "Ladies and gentlemen! Our Principal, Mrs. Wanda Hare!" he shouted into the microphone, causing the applause to boom even more.

As the players approached the two in the middle, they formed a circle around Wanda and Coach. Everyone put their hand in the middle of the circle, and Coach once again put the microphone to his mouth. "Panthers on three! One... Two... Three!" he shouted, followed by an eruption from the players and the entire stadium shouting 'PANTHERS!'.

Wanda made her way back to the bleachers when she spotted George and Michelle standing by the gate, just outside of the field. Wanda smiled, wondering if they had been there for her speech. As she made her way to her husband and daughter, she glanced into the stands to see Katherine pushing her way through the crowd to make her way down to where Wanda was.

"Hunny, tha' was one o' the bes' speeches I ev'r did hear," George smiled, wrapping his arms around his wife's neck as she exited the field.

"How long have you been here?" Wanda asked as she embraced the warmth of her husband under the cool air biting away at her.

"Mommy! Mommy! We've been here since you walked onto the field! I tried to call for you before you got out there, but Daddy stopped me," Michelle said, rolling her eyes and looking up at her dad. Knowing that she and George had been there during the entire speech made Wanda happy. She may not have known they were there, but she believed their presence gave her the confidence she desired to deliver the speech so well.

"I'm so daggone prouda ya, Hunny," George smiled, releasing his hug and putting his hand on top of Michelle's head. As the words came out of his mouth, Katherine came running up to the crowd.

"Mrs. Hare! That was totally awesome!" Katherine yelled, out of breath, as she arrived. "You lit this stadium up! Do you feel you've accomplished your goal now?"

Wanda laughed and pointed at George and Michelle. "Katherine, this is my husband, George, and my daughter, Michelle."

"Oh, it is such a pleasure to meet you both!" Katherine said, reaching her hand out towards George and then leaning in to give Michelle a hug. "Your Mommy is one amazing woman," she whispered to Michelle.

"I know," Michelle started. "She deals with my Daddy."

George shot Michelle a look and glanced back up to Katherine. "Tha's very kind o' ya, Ms..."

"Church. Katherine Church!" She beamed with pride. "Well, I'm going to go stretch my legs until the game starts again. Will I see you back in the bleachers?"

Wanda looked over at George, who gave a subtle nod. "We'll be there, Katherine," Wanda smiled.

Chapter 5
Children Will Be Children

Michelle looked out the window of her fifth grade classroom. She had drowned out her History teacher going on about the Civil War and the root cause of it. The memory of her mother's powerful speech, weeks ago, and the crowd's rousing applause, stayed with her. Her mother was a source of both pride and inspiration for her.

"Michelle, are you still with us?" the teacher called from the front of the classroom.

"Yes, Mr. Lee. I'm sorry," she replied, looking back at her teacher, her face flushed. "I'm sorry, Sir, I was thinking about why the Confederate Army would have betrayed the rest of the United States," she lied.

"Ah, excellent question," the teacher started as he went into a lecture based on Michelle's made up inquisition.

Michelle looked back down at her paper and pretended to take notes, when in reality she was scribbling her mother's speech from memory. Her favorite line was when her mother ended her speech and said *'Finally, I urge all of you, players and students alike, to enjoy your life, the precious moments you have.'* Her mother had a way with words, one that she had not inherited.

As the bell rang, Michelle packed her stuff. A red-headed boy named Charlie approached her desk and snatched her notepad from underneath her book bag. "Well, well, well. What do we have here?"

"Give it back Charlie, that's mine," Michelle calmly said.

"Enjoy your life. Precious moments," he mocked as he read the words scribbled on the paper. "What is this?"

"Give it back, Charlie," she groaned. "It was what my Mom said at her first football game."

"Oh, your Mommy," he said, pretending to be crying and rubbing balled up fist underneath his eyes. "I know who your Mommy is. My Daddy told me all about her.

Said she's a real tool, she don't belong in the Principal spot."

"Charlie, leave me alone. Please," Michelle begged. She felt her face heat up as her cheeks flushed red.

"Why are you acting like such a crybaby? Boo-hoo, Mommy this, Mommy that. Your Mama ain't nothin' but a bitch."

WHAP!

Michelle had reared her hand back and thrown a punch directly between Charlie's eyes, causing a stream of blood to flow out of his nose. She wasn't sure what came over her, but she knew it felt good to teach him a lesson.

"You bitch!" Charlie shouted, his hand cupped under his nose, collecting a pool of blood.

"Michelle Hare! What in the world do you think you're doing, young lady?" Mr. Lee called as his tall and lanky figure bustled into the classroom from the hallway.

"He called my mom the b-word, Sir."

"You're a liar!" Charlie called out, pointing his other finger at her accusingly.

"I don't want to hear it. Michelle, go to the office. Now. Charlie, come with me and I'll take you to the Nurse."

Michelle looked down at her feet and began shuffling to the office. She knew she was going to be in trouble, maybe even suspended. Regardless, she refused to let anyone speak ill of her mom.

Accompanied by Mr. Lee, she entered the Office. Charlie followed in behind her. She sat down on the couch in the Office and waited for Mr. Lee to finish tending to Charlie in the Nurse's office. "Now young lady, come with me," he said as he exited the Nurse's office.

"Yes, Sir," she said as she stood up and followed him to the Principal's office. When they arrived, she saw the bald head and clean-shaven face of her Principal writing away on a piece of paper. As Mr. Lee lightly rapped on the door, the Principal looked up from his papers to see the pair standing in his doorway.

"Ms. Hare, Mr. Lee. To what do I owe the pleasure?" he smiled.

"Not the pleasure today, Sir." Mr. Lee started as he nudged Michelle into the office. As he sat down in the empty chair beside Michelle, he continued. "Michelle here punched another student in the face, nearly breaking his nose."

The Principal's eyes got wide as he cocked his head slightly to the side, stunned by the words he had just heard. "I'm sorry, Ms. Hare punched another student?"

"Yes sir," Michelle piped up. "He stole my notebook and started making fun of me and called my mom a b-word."

"Ms. Hare, you know we don't tolerate violence here. I'm going to have to call your parents."

As George arrived at the school to pick up his daughter, he couldn't imagine what would have possessed his innocent, sweet little girl to punch a boy in the face. She had inherited her mother's patience and ability to stay calm during tough moments, so an outburst like this was a rarity.

Walking into the Main Office, he glanced over to the Nurse's office where he saw a red-headed boy with a crimson stained rag held to his nose. "*Mus' be the boy she clocked,*" he chuckled to himself. "I'm here to pick up 'Chelle Hare," he grunted as he approached the front desk.

"And how are you related to her?" The receptionist asked.

"I'm 'er Daddy," George responded.

The receptionist got up and made her way into the back offices. After several minutes, she returned, followed by the principal and Michelle. "Hunny, what in the world didja do?" he asked as she came into sight.

"He called Mommy the b-word!" Michelle cried out.

"He what?!" George exclaimed, looking back at the Principal with anger building up within. George was very different than Michelle and Wanda in the sense that he often couldn't contain his anger. "I sure as hell hope ya gonna be punishin' 'at boy too, Sir."

"Mr. Hare, please. We don't use that kind of language here," the Principal said. He immediately regretted upsetting George and was attempting to calm him down. "Look, they were the only two in the classroom when this happened. He claims that he never said that, that she approached him and started bullying him. The condition of the poor boy's nose makes his story more believable than hers at this point."

"So, if that lil boy woulda touched my daughter inappropriately, you'da still b'lieved him o'er 'er cause there ain't no 'proof'? I don' condone you punching him 'Chelle, but I also don' condone you, Sir," George said, turning his attention to the Principal and pointing his strong, tanned finger. The angrier he got, the more his country dialect came out. "Not punishin' 'at lil boy. 'Cause my lil girl isa girl, y'all 'cided to believe 'im ov'r 'er? No lookin' into it, nothin'. I'll be talkin' to the School Board 'bout this, Sir. You have you'self a nice day." George said, as he took Michelle's hand and turned to leave.

George was stewing over what had just transpired when they reached his pickup truck. He opened the door for his daughter to let her slide in and made his way around the truck into the driver's side. George got in the truck without a word and took off.

"I'm sorry, Daddy," Michelle spoke up after several long and silent minutes.

"Hunny," George started as he reached one hand over to hold his daughter's. "You ain't done a thing wrong. You was defending yer mama. I ain't happy you hada punch him, but I get it, baby. I'm mo' mad at the school for 'llowin' that boy to get off scot-free."

George had to take a deep breath to contain his emotions again. "You're only outta school for the resta the day. Which means ya getta help me in the garden the resta day."

"Okay, Daddy," Michelle said, trying to hide a smile. Michelle enjoyed helping her dad in the garden, so she didn't look at this as much of a punishment. Neither did George.

"Baby," George said.

"Yes, Daddy?"

"Le's keep this a secret 'tween you an' me," Michelle slowly nodded. She knew why without him saying it. Her mother's worst fear had come true, and they didn't want to make her step down from her position.

Chapter 6

Exam Week

M onths had passed since Wanda had found a new sense of courage within herself at the first football game of the year. Until now, her career as Principal had been smooth sailing. Coach and the staff were slowly starting to respect her, students supported her, and the community showed overwhelming support. She felt amazing.

Exams were just around the corner as Wanda prepared for the antics and actions students may pull to get out of exams. Many students fake sickness, play hooky, and even intentionally get in fights just to avoid taking exams when they are scheduled. It was a fun and interesting time for Wanda, her first round of exams under her careful watch as the Principal.

A knock came at the door as Wanda looked up from her desk to see Katherine standing at the door. Katherine had been Wanda's work-study student for a while and had performed exceptionally well. She was thorough, paid careful attention to detail, and really took pride in her work. Many work-study students used the program to get out of work, but Katherine seemed to use it to increase her workload and responsibilities. "Come on in, Sweetie," Wanda beamed.

"Hi Mrs. Wanda! I finished filling out the paperwork you asked me to start on last week. Whew! It was a lot!"

"Katherine, I'm so proud of your work ethic! I'm sure going to miss you as a work study student next semester." Wanda took the papers from Katherine and began looking through them to double-check Katherine's work.

Katherine looked down at her feet as she said, "Oh," she said, disappointed.

"What's wrong, Katherine?" Wanda asked as she looked up from the stack of papers. She made eye contact with Katherine, looking into her icy blue eyes.

"I've just been learning a lot from you this semester and was hoping...Well, I was hoping I could continue next semester." Katherine confessed.

"Katherine, I wish you could! You've been a real help around here and have provided me with some great company. But you know you must take an extra curriculum course next semester so you can graduate on time. I don't want to hold you back from your full potential, because you can accomplish anything you set your mind too, Sweetie," Wanda said, hoping her words would break the frown that had formed across Katherine's face.

Wanda truly wished that Katherine could continue being her work study student, but she knew she had to put Katherine's best interest first. "Now, I don't want you to think you didn't do a good enough job here. You have been a great help, and I don't know what I'm going to do without you!"

"Thank you, Mrs. Wanda. I really appreciate that. I hope it's okay if I continue to stop by?" she replied, a smile slowly creeping back onto her face.

"You know it is sweetie!" Wanda said, as the bell rang to signal the end of first period. "I would be disappointed if you didn't."

Wanda shot up from her desk as the commotion from outside of her office got louder and louder. The shuffle and bustle of kids running rang through the hallways, the chants of kids bellowed throughout the Main Office. As Wanda reached the door leading to the hallway, she saw a group of students standing in a circle. She instantly knew what was going on: people were fighting.

"Hey! Hey!" Wanda called as she tried to push her way through the wall of students surrounding the fight. "Move! Get out of the way. Come on, y'all!"

Wanda heard a whistle blowing from down the hallway. She turned her head and saw Robert running down the hallway towards the commotion. Wanda continued to push her way through the sea of students, now swallowing her alive. As she pushed through the last wave to stand in the ring the two students were fighting in, she called out, "Boys! Enough! Enough!" Neither the students surrounding the fight, nor the boys' fighting, paid her any mind.

She glanced around to see where Robert was and noticed him simply standing outside of the circle. *"Why is he just standing there,"* she thought to herself as she turned her attention back to the fighting students. She recognized one student as a wrestler, pitted against a football player. She knew she had to do something before someone got seriously hurt.

"Alright boys, enough," she said, reaching out to grab the wrestler's large shoulder to get his attention.

Her small hand barely wrapped around the three-hundred-pound wrestler's shoulder. As her hand contacted the navy varsity jacket of the boy, he slung around, shoving Wanda to the ground.

Wanda's head contacted the ground, instantly sending a ringing sensation throughout her ears and head. Everything fell silent, but Wanda didn't know if it was because she had hit her head or if the hallway was quieting down.

"Shit, shit, shit!" the wrestler called as he looked at what he had just done.

"Dude, what the hell?" the football player called out as he got off the floor, jaw dropped and eyes wide.

"Man, I didn't mean to. I swear I didn't mean to!" He said, turning back around to where Wanda was laying.

Wanda's vision was becoming blurry as the pain erupted from the back of her head to behind her eyes. She tried to prop herself up on her elbow and look around to see where Robert was. As she glanced around, she became dizzy, but spotted Robert in the same spot he had been in before. Wanda dropped back to the floor, unable to hold herself up any longer. She lay there, staring out at the ceiling.

"Come on Mrs. Hare, stay with me!" the football player pushed past the wrestler who was holding his hand to his mouth. "I got you, I got you," the boy started, kneeling down as he took off his jacket and pressed it against the back of Wanda's bleeding head. "Someone get help!"

Robert began pushing his way through the students, moving them by loudly blowing his whistle in the ears of students standing in his way. "Move! Move! Move!" he called out. As he approached the center of the circle, he could hear Deputy Cooke shouting at the wrestler to stay where he was.

The wrestler, scared of the consequences of his now brutal actions, turned to run. He tried to push through the inner wall of the circle, but the students all locked their hands together, effectively blocking his path. Deputy Cooke easily broke through the crowd of students and immediately handcuffed the wrestler against the wall.

"Get back to your damn classes, now, or I'll have you all in handcuffs next! Move it!" Deputy Cooke shouted. The students quickly obeyed, dismissing themselves from the action and making their way back to their assigned classrooms. "Wanda, Wanda, are you okay?" he said as he kneeled beside Robert and the football player to tend to Wanda.

Robert had already pulled out his cellphone to call an ambulance to the school as he watched Wanda lay on the floor, the football player's once navy jacket now turning to a crimson black. "Come on Wanda, stay with us," he called, watching her slowly close and open her eyes.

Wanda opened her eyes and held them open as she turned to look at the football player holding the jacket to her head. "Thank... you..." she slowly said, trying to lift herself up once again.

"No, no, lay back down Wanda," Robert said, guiding her back into a lying position gently.

Wanda began to black out as she heard running boots come through the door of the school. She slowly tried to keep her eyes open but didn't keep them open much after the EMS took over for the trio who had helped her.

Wanda slowly opened her eyes, the dull pain of a hammer banging her head repeatedly flooding back. The constant beeping of the monitors attached to her arms rang in her ears alongside the hammering pain. The fluorescent lights above her shone deep into Wanda's eyes. She immediately turned her head to the side to avoid the burning light. In turning her head, she saw the football player sitting next to her.

"Mrs. Hare! You're up," he said, standing up from his chair and walking to where she was laying. "I am so sorry about what happened."

"Chad... It's Chad, right?"

"Yes ma'am."

"Don't apologize, you helped me before anyone else could get there," Wanda said weakly. "I am disappointed in you fighting, however." Chad slowly nodded his head and looked down at his feet. "But I will excuse it because you saved me. Also, your new varsity jacket is on me."

"Look, I'm sorry he did that to you. I'm sorry we were fighting, too. I accidentally bumped him in the hallway and instead of walking away, I returned the yells he was throwing out at me. Then it escalated, so I completely understand if I get detention," Chad finished as Robert walked through the door with a cup of coffee and a cup of water. Robert sat the water beside Wanda's bed and turned to Chad.

"I'm glad you're accepting of that, because you're going to have out-of-school suspension for a week," Robert said sternly.

"No, Robert. He will have three days of in-school suspension." Wanda rolled her head towards Robert and said, "He leapt into action after I was injured."

"But Ma'am..."

"No buts, Robert. This boy helped make sure the injury didn't turn out worse. What were you doing, Robert? You stood in the same place after they knocked me down and didn't make your way through until after Chad here helped me," she said in an accusing tone.

"Ma'am..." Robert started.

"We will talk about this later, Robert. Now Chad, why aren't you in school, young man?"

"Well, honestly, I wanted to make sure you were okay," he admitted. "I kinda left school without telling anyone, but I was really worried about you."

"Thank you, Honey, I'm fine," Wanda said with an unconvincing smile. "Just a headache right now." She reached to the back of her head and felt the five new staples that had been inserted. "And a few staples. Head back home, take the rest of the day off. I expect to see you tomorrow, at the in-school suspension room."

"Yes, Ma'am," Chad said as he turned around to leave. As he made his way through the door, Wanda turned her attention back to Robert.

"What of the other young man? Elliot, I believe?"

"Deputy Cooke took him into custody as soon as he got there. The boy tried to run, but a group of students stepped up to stop him until Cooke could get there," Robert informed her as he sat down beside her bed. "Do you want to press charges on him, Ma'am?"

"No Robert, I don't. I expect to have him suspended for the rest of the semester, repeating his classes next semester. The fight was a minor interruption, probably only meant to get one of them out of exams. He can miss those exams, but he will pay for it. He'll have to double his class load to graduate on time."

"Ma'am, I'm sorry I wasn't there sooner," Robert half-heartedly said. "I couldn't make it through the students in time."

"Robert, enough," Wanda snapped, having heard enough of his excuses for his actions that day. "You did not try to get through the crowd until *AFTER* they knocked me to the ground. Mind telling me what the hesitation was? Because I'm not going to lie to you Robert, I am highly disappointed in you."

As Robert opened his mouth to talk, the door of her room swung open, interrupting him. "Hunny! Hunny!" George yelled, pushing his way past Robert. "Golly honey, arya okay?"

"I'm fine George, I'm fine. Just a few staples," Wanda laughed, as she leaned up slowly to show George the staples on the back of her head. "Robert, you can leave now. We will continue this discussion another day." Robert put his head down and slowly turned around to make his way out of the hospital room.

"Where is Michelle at?" Wanda questioned, laying her head back down on the fluffy hospital bed pillow.

But before George could answer, Michelle flew through the door and ran to her mother. She grabbed her hand and started kissing it. "Oh Mommy, I was so worried! Are you okay?"

"Yer Mama is fine, 'Chelle. She gon'a be a little sore the next couple-a days. Im'a need you to help around the house a little mo' 'till yer Mama gets to feelin' better," George said, putting his arm around his daughter's quaint shoulers. "Look at the back of 'er head, baby."

Wanda slowly lifted her head up and turned the back of it toward Michelle. "Oh my gosh, Mommy! That looks like it hurts!"

"I'm fine, baby, I promise," she smiled at George and Michelle.

The hospital wanted to keep Wanda overnight to watch for any symptoms of a concussion. George made his way back home to get a bag of necessities together and to drop Michelle off at Josiah and Joanne's house for the night. George looked over at Michelle, who was staring quietly out of the window of the moving truck.

"'Chelle? You okay, baby? Worried 'bout yer Mama?" George asked, as he reached over to grab his daughter's hand.

"Daddy," she started, turning to look at her dad's naturally suntanned face. "Is this going to happen to Mommy a lot?"

"Oh, heavens no, baby. Yer Mama likely won' ev'n see another situation like this again. She'sa tough one, yer Mama. Jus' like you," he said, turning to her and winking. "She's-a gon' be jus' fine, baby."

"Daddy, why can't I stay with you and Mommy tonight?"

"Honey, you know you got school 'morrow. Yer gran'daddy and gran'ma are gon' make sure you get to school in the mornin'."

"Daddy, I'm worried about Mommy," Michelle pouted as she moved her hand from her dad's and crossed her arms across her chest. She looked down at the floorboard, littered with empty Pepsi cans and Nab wrappers. "It's not fair that you get to be there, and I don't. She's my Mommy!"

"'Chelle, calm down now, Baby. Yer Mama is gon' be home 'morrow 'fore you get home from school." George knew this was hard on their daughter. He was afraid that if Wanda knew how upset she was, she might step down from her position. In truth, Michelle knew the same thing, so she didn't say anything in front of her mother.

"Promise, Daddy?"

"Promise baby," George said, leaning over to wipe a tear from her eye.

Wanda lay in her hospital bed, silently watching the daily news playing across the boxy TV hung up in her room. As a story about a local monkey escaping the zoo came across the screen, a soft knock came from the door. She rolled her head over to see Katherine coming through the door.

"Oh, Mrs. Wanda! I was so worried. I came as soon as school got out," she said, nearly running to her bedside. She leaned down and wrapped her arms around Wanda, immediately backing away, fearing she had hurt Wanda in some way. "I'm so sorry. I was just worried. I shouldn't have hugged you!"

Wanda chuckled. "You're fine Katherine. Sit, sit," she said, motioning her head towards the chair on the opposite side of the room. "How did you get in without supervision?"

Katherine blushed. "I kind of snuck in." To quickly change the subject, she continued. "OH! I saw Craig getting out of his car when I pulled up, I think he stopped at the vend..." and before Katherine could finish, Craig came through the door holding an open bottle of Coke and a bouquet with a 'Get Well Soon' card poking out the side.

"Mrs. Wanda, how are you feeling? Are you okay? I'm so sorry this happened..." Craig trailed off as he saw the back of her head. "Oh my God, is that from today?"

"Yes, but I'm fine, really. I appreciate both of you coming by to see me. Are those for me or Katherine?" Wanda said, jokingly pointing towards the flowers.

Craig, turning red in the face and looking over at Katherine, who was also turning red, said, "They're for you, Ma'am. They're from Katherine and me. We both went in on the flowers when we heard what happened," he said, setting the beautiful mix of roses and sunflowers down on the table beside her bed. Craig made his way to the seat beside Katherine and sat down.

"I can't believe he did that!" said Katherine. She showed a hint of anger that Wanda had never seen in her before. "He probably thinks that he can just push you around because you're a woman! I bet if Mr. Kane had been there, it never would have happened. So disrespectful!"

"Look, I know that guy and I think she's right, Mrs. Wanda. He can be a real prick. Excuse my language. He's always bad-mouthing you for being a woman," Craig chipped in. Wanda noticed a hint of anger in his voice, too.

"Katherine, Craig, it's fine. I knew by taking this job that there would be students like that. Did I ever think one of them would accidentally put me in the hospital? Not at all," she laughed again. This time, she laughed a little too hard as her head started pounding again.

Katherine and Craig noticed her wincing and turned to look at each other with concerned faces. Finally,

Craig turned back to look at Wanda and said, "When do you think you'll be back? A lot of the students are worried about you."

"You really are loved by most of the school, Ma'am," Katherine added.

Wanda smiled at the sentiment of the two students. "I'm not sure when I'll be back in. I'm hoping I'll be back on Wednesday. I know I won't be back tomorrow. Who knows when they'll release me."

The three sat in silence for another thirty minutes, watching an episode of *Jeopardy!* Before Katherine and Craig said their goodbyes and got up to leave. As they made their way through the door, Allison made her way through the open door and beside Wanda's bedside.

"Oh dear! How are you doing, Wanda?" she asked, pulling a chair closer to the bedside. "I wish I would have been there to help you. I'm so sorry!" Tears were slowly forming in her eyes.

"Honey," Wanda started, reaching over and placing her hand on Allison's. "There was nothing anyone could have done to prevent that. I wouldn't have wanted you and I both hurt."

"Oh Wanda," Allison chirped. "The entire faculty has been asking about you all day! Even Coach came by to ask if we had heard anything about you."

"Coach? Wow, that's an unexpected person to care that much." Wanda thought to herself. "That is very kind of them. I plan on being back on Wednesday."

"Ma'am, please don't rush back. Robert can handle your duties until you're healed and well."

The mention of Robert's name sent a chill down Wanda's spine. She still couldn't understand why Robert remained outside the crowd. Remembering everything that happened before she got knocked down was tough, but one thing stood out: the look in Robert's eyes when she spotted him at the edge of the crowd. He had an almost vile look in his eyes, like he wanted to see her get hurt. She couldn't place it exactly, but she felt like he had intentionally stayed out of it until she got hurt.

"No, I'll be back on Wednesday. Allison," she said, turning to look at Allison with worry in her eyes. "I'm not sure Robert didn't intentionally stay outside of the crowd. Even when I got knocked down, it took him a while to get through the crowd. Something isn't right."

The look on Allison's face said what her mouth couldn't. She was stunned at the accusation, but then slowly faded into an 'aha!' moment. "Now that you mention it, he seemed off when he got back to school today. He was angry, but it almost seemed like he was relishing in his temporary moment of power. You don't think..."

"Maybe." Wanda said, understanding what she meant without waiting for Allison to finish her sentence.

Chapter 7
Smoking in the Bathroom

The new semester had started a few days after Wanda had the staples removed from the back of her head. She was finally feeling free of the constraint that held together the back of her head. She rolled her neck as she sat at her desk doing paperwork. A series of pops followed through her movements. Just what she needed.

Suddenly, she caught a whiff of something. Wanda had always had a keen sense of smell. Even from a young age, she was the first to know when dinner was ready by smell and smell alone. She was like a hound dog in the way she would stick her nose up in the air and sniff. Cigarette smoke. Coming from her school? Wanda wouldn't have that.

She pushed her chair back and sprung to action. Power walking through the hallways with her nose in the air, Wanda was on the hunt for where the smell of cigarette smoke was coming from. She recognized the putrid smell of nicotine-infused tobacco swarming throughout her school. The closer to the smell she got, the more pungent the smell got to her.

Eventually, she got to the boy's bathroom in one of the wings adjacent to the Main Office. She could see the smoke billowing out of the bottom of the bathroom door. Wanda's face turned a furious red and she stomped her foot. *"Not on my watch,"* she thought to herself.

She marched to the bathroom and knocked on the door. The sound of feet shuffling, and a window opening could be heard through the door. Wanda flung the door open to see three boys attempting to climb out the high window in the bathroom.

"Ahem." Wanda crossed her arms and stared down the boys. One boy in a Motörhead shirt was holding the side of another boy in a black shirt with skulls and crossbones on it, who was standing on a third. A boy who was on all fours, wearing a dark blue shirt.

The Motörhead boy turned around and Wanda recognized him as Jesus Reaquiz. His gray eyes went big, and he let go of the skulls and crossbones boy. The skull and crossbones boy fell, his long black hair covering his face as he hit the ground. Wanda looked down at him and shook her head. "*Mike Kramer,*" she thought to herself. The boy on all fours slowly stood up and turned to face Wanda. He ran a hand across his shaved brown head and his blue eyes glanced away from Wanda's gaze.

"Quentin Randolph," Wanda started as she looked at Quentin brushing off his blue shirt. "Mike Kramer, Jesus Reaquiz. Anybody mind telling me..." Wanda paused and lifted her nose to the air taking in a deep whiff of the repulsive smell. She scrunched her nose and looked back at the boys. "...Why I smell cigarette smoke coming from this bathroom?" She crossed her arms and began tapping her foot as she awaited their answer.

Quentin looked at the boy standing next to him and the boy laying on the other side then back at Wanda. "No, Ma'am, it smelled like that when we came in here." Mike's eyes went wide at the lie his friend had told. He slowly stood and looked over at Quentin and tried to subtly shake his head 'no'.

"Is that right?" Wanda asked, with her eyebrows raised and her bottom lip out. "Then why was there smoke coming from under the bathroom door?" Wanda asked, hoping the boys would be truthful after the undeniable evidence that they had been caught.

"Uh…" Jesus started. "Well, I think what you were seeing was dust and dirt." Jesus lied. Wanda raised an eyebrow and cocked her head to the side. "See, we were cleaning the bathroom." Mike looked over at Jesus and his eyes went wide as he turned his head to the side and gave his friend a 'really, man?' look.

Quentin spoke up next, "Yeah, we're really good students. We believe in helping the school."

Wanda chuckled. "You boys have as much potential as anybody in this school," she began, her gaze glancing across the lineup. "However, I know from my teaching days that you don't apply them for the right reasons. Don't get me wrong, I believe people can change.

"But if you were cleaning the bathroom, as you say, and the bathroom smelled like smoke when you got in here, then you did nothing wrong."

The two boys that lied nodded, but Mike gulped instead. "However," Wanda continued as she killed the boy's hopes of getting off scot-free. "Can anybody explain why you were trying to climb out the bathroom window? Mike, maybe, this time?"

Sweat dripped down the pimply face of the pale boy. He shifted uncomfortably as he looked at his friends and back at Wanda. "Okay, it was us," he said as he fell to his knees and put his hands together to beg for forgiveness. "If I get in trouble again, my dad will kick me out of the house."

Wanda frowned. She didn't want to kick the boys out of school for this, but she knew they needed to be punished somehow. Except maybe Mike, who had been the only one not to lie to her. "Mike, you're getting a lesser punishment for telling me the truth and not lying to me. One day of in-school suspension."

Mike jumped up and ran to Wanda and hugged her stiff body as she leaned her head back to be as far away from Mike's face as possible. "That's enough," she finally said as she pushed him away.

"Yes, Ma'am," was all Mike could say before pausing and turned around to face his friends. 'Sorry' he mouthed to them.

"As for you two," Wanda said as she directed her attention back to Jesus and Quentin. "You will face a bit more of a severe punishment for continuing with the lies. We will discuss punishment for the three of you, immediately, in my office."

"Yes, Ma'am," the boys said in unison as they hung their heads.

Wanda scribbled something across her notepad as she looked up at Jesus and Quentin. "I am very disappointed in both of you," she said with disappointment stricken across her face. Her bottom lip came back in as she continued, "You will both be facing one week of in-school suspension. I expect to see you in the detention hall every day next week."

Both boys looked at one another and back at Wanda before shaking their heads in understanding. "Ma'am?" Quentin said.

"Yes, Quentin," Wanda said as she raised an eyebrow.

"For what it is worth, I'm sorry," he said as he looked down at his feet in shame.

"May I ask," Wanda said as she laid her pen down and leaned back in her chair. "Why do you boys smoke cigarettes?" Wanda glanced back at the open files on her desk for each of the boys and quirked an eyebrow when she realized all three of them were supposed to be in the same class right now. "You know they're terrible for you, which you would know from Health class."

Quentin shrugged. "I don't know, it just seemed like a cool thing to do at the time," Quentin confessed. He sighed and looked back up at Wanda. "I started a few years ago and can't quit now. It's addicting."

"Again," Wanda said with a frown. "Had you boys been in Health class, you would have known that nicotine is an addictive substance."

"It helps with my stress, though," Mike finally spoke up. "It helps me chill out when I have high stress situations."

"What could be so high stress when you aren't in class?" Wanda narrowed her eyes on Mike.

"I have a lot going on at home, okay?" Mike snapped before looking away from Wanda.

Wanda frowned and glanced at the solemn expression on Mike's face. Wanda hadn't considered that maybe he was acting out because of his home life. In fact, that could have been-and sounded like it was for Mike-the reason all three boys acted out.

She nodded. "I understand, Mike, and I am sorry you are going through that." Mike chanced a glance back at Wanda with a look of curiosity in his gaze. "If you ever need to talk, I and the guidance counselor are here for you."

Wanda's conversation with the troublesome boys was interrupted by a knock on the door. Wanda quirked an eyebrow and looked over to the closed door. "Come back in a few, I'm busy with students right now," she called out to the new visitor. and turned back to the boys.

Instead of leaving, the visitor opened the door, despite Wanda's request. Robert poked his head in and looked at Mike, Jesus, and Quentin. "Sorry to bother you, Wanda..."

"Mrs. Hare in front of the students, please, Mr. Kan e..."

"*Mrs. Hare,*" Robert spat with sarcasm. Wanda raised her eyebrows and blinked a few times. She was stunned at his sarcasm and utter disrespect. "What exactly is going on? I would like to be more involved with the students."

Wanda stared at Robert, gape-jawed. "Mr. Kane, I believe I can handle these students by myself. Perhaps next time, we can handle it together."

"No, I think it needs to be now," Robert said, rolling his eyes and looking at the boys. "Boys, what are you in here for?"

"They were caught smoking in the bathroom, Mr. Kane," Wanda said as she leaned forward. "Please address your questions to me."

"I'm talking to the students, *Mrs. Hare.*"

"Mr. Kane," Wanda said as she stood up. "I need you to leave this office, at this moment."

"Boys, you're free to leave," Robert said. The boys stood up to leave.

Wanda put her hand out to stop the boys from getting up. "They have not received their detention slips yet, Mr. Kane."

He laughed. "Those won't be necessary," Robert said, as he glanced back at Wanda. "They got caught doing something most adults can do. Besides, these boys are eighteen, and they're old enough to smoke if they want to."

Wanda ground her teeth together as she narrowed her eyes on Robert and leaned on her desk. "I will not allow smoking on this campus," Wanda stated. "These boys have too bright of a future to look forward to. They have no time to kill themselves with cigarettes."

Mike and Quentin looked at one another. They had never been talked about like that before. Normally teachers and school staff called them 'hopeless causes' or told them they had 'no chance to graduate'. Both boys blinked back a tear as they looked back at Wanda.

"I'll take my punishment," Quentin said.

"Yeah," Jesus followed. "I think I deserve mine."

"Me too," Mike said, staring Robert down.

Wanda smiled at the boys and sat down to finish filling out their detention slips. She slid them across the table to the boys. "You're all dismissed." She turned her attention back to Robert. "You can stay. Oh, and boys? Please close the door on your way out." The boys nodded and took their slips, standing up and hurrying out of the office. They closed the door behind them, and the room was hauntingly silent. You could feel the tension in the air as Robert and Wanda gazed at one another.

"Robert," Wanda started as she shook her head. "How dare you undermine me in front of the students like that?"

"I don't think smoking is that big of a deal, especially for eighteen-year-olds." Robert scoffed. "I smoke and it hasn't killed me yet. That whole 'killing people' narrative is part of a political scheme to kill the tobacco industry."

Wanda was seeing a new side of Robert, and it wasn't a side that she necessarily liked. In fact, it was nearly repulsive. "Robert, it has been proven that smoking kills people. My daddy was a tobacco farmer, and he stopped once he realized his products were being used to make things that killed people. He felt like he had blood on his hands.

"I would feel that way if I *didn't* punish those boys for lying and smoking. They wouldn't learn if we weren't here to guide them in the right direction. Any Principal has the principles to know that."

"Are you saying I'm not cut out to be a principal?" Robert spat as he took a step forward and leaned into Wanda's face.

"That isn't what I'm saying at all, but if the shoe f its..." Wanda had had enough of the blatant and utter disrespect Robert was showing her. "What I am saying, however, is that it is our job as educators to uphold the rules. We shouldn't allow something harmful to people's health on this campus just because you personally take part in that activity or think it's okay."

Robert stood back up and brushed off his clothes. "I think we are done here, Wanda." Robert turned around and walked to the door. As he opened the door, Wanda called out to him.

Wanda pulled her Mustang into the garage of her brick home. She got out and gathered her briefcase out of the back seat. Before she could get turned around, she felt a small set of arms wrap around her waist. She smiled and looked down at Michelle, resting her head on Wanda's hip.

"I missed you, Mommy." Michelle squeezed her mother as tight as she could.

"Oh honey," Wanda started as she pat Michelle on the head. "I missed you more than you know."

The garage door opened, and George walked out, leaning against the hood of Wanda's car. He looked at his wife and frowned as he instantly recognized the look of subtle stress stricken across his wife's small face. "'Chelle, why 'on't you head on 'side so I can talk to yer Mama."

Michelle pouted and looked up at her mother. "Do I have to, Mommy?"

Wanda let a weak smile plague her lips as she tried to convince her only daughter that she was okay. "Yes honey," she said as she kissed her forehead. "I need to talk to Daddy, okay?"

Michelle huffed and let go of her mother so she could cross her arms. "Fine." She stomped away and let the screen door slam behind her.

George looked from the door back to Wanda. "'Swrong, hon?"

Wanda sighed and looked down at her feet. She shifted her weight from one side to the other. "I got into a heated discussion with Robert today."

George's eyes went wide, and his jaw dropped. "Whatcha mean, Wanda?"

She looked back up and into George's caring eyes. She felt at ease when she looked at him. "He undermined and disrespected me in front of some students who I was giving detention to."

"He did what?" George said. He stomped his foot and crossed his arms. "Why I oughta..."

"It was bad, George," Wanda admitted, feeling ashamed of how he had treated her. "He did everything but call me names in front of the students. Maybe I'm not cut out for this job."

"Nonsense!" George said as he walked towards his wife. He took her in his arms and pulled her close to him. "Lis'n to me, dear. You's the bes' damn principal I ever seen."

Wanda weakly smiled and rested her head on her husband's chest. She felt warmth in his embrace, almost like the hard day she'd had, and all its troubles were but a mere memory now. Almost.

"I feel like nobody respects me because I'm a woman." She sadly sighed. "It's hard to do this, George."

"When 'ave you ev'r back'd down from-a challenge?" George asked her and looked down at the top of her head. He planted a kiss on the top of her dark hair.

"George," she said as she turned her head up to face him. She stared into his strong eyes and chiseled face. "Do you really think I can do this?"

"No," he said bluntly. Wanda's face dropped at her husband's words. "I *know* ya can."

Chapter 8

Anonymous

Wanda sat hunched over her desk, filling out the latest school's progress report. After each semester, she reviewed the school's performance to ensure it met the standards. Besides that report, the District Office wanted her to put together an action plan to round out the school's progress report.

Wanda's phone rang, breaking her attention from the progress report. She looked down and frowned when she saw the District Office number. Calls from the District Office were never fun. They were all business, just like this pesky progress report.

"Hello?" Wanda said as she lifted the receiver to her ear.

"Wanda," Shawn Carlile said from the other side of the phone. His tone was one that caused Wanda concern. "Do you have a few minutes to chat?"

Wanda laid her pen down and leaned back in her chair. "Sure, Shawn. What's on your mind?"

"Well..." Shawn paused. He clicked his tongue and began again. "The Administrative Department has received a few complaints about you over the last few weeks."

Wanda's heart dropped to her stomach. She couldn't believe the words coming out of his mouth. There hadn't been any parents that she had confrontations with, and the faculty seemed to love Wanda, except for Coach. And now, Robert...

"Which student is this involving?" she finally asked.

"I can't tell you," he said, with a slight sigh at the end.

"Right, confidentiality."

"No, Wanda," Shawn corrected. "The complaints have all been anonymous. No name, no reference to students, just that you aren't qualified to be Principal."

Wanda blinked back a tear as the words coming out of the phone receiver stung her soul. She was now sweating as the panic that she may lose her job over this set in. She had spent her entire career working so hard to get to this point. Without this job, she would feel like a lost cause.

"What's my punishment, Shawn?" Wanda asked.

Shawn chuckled. Wanda blinked twice and looked over at the phone receiver. "No, Wanda," he started before taking a breath. "I just wanted to bring this to your attention. We aren't taking them too seriously because they've all been anonymous written letters. Very short letters at that, two sentences at most. They read things like 'Wanda is unqualified to be principal' and 'Wanda Hare is endangering our children. She is unfit to be principal.'"

A wave of relief washed over Wanda like a calm surrender. She sighed and smiled before leaning back in her chair. "Thank you, Shawn."

"Don't thank me yet," he said as his voice turned more solemn. "I can only stave off the School Board for so long. If too many of these complaints come in, or worse yet, some of them go to individual Board members, we could have a problem."

Wanda's moment of relief ended, and she leaned back up. She rested her forehead in her left hand as her right held the receiver to her ear. "I just don't understand, Shawn."

"Wanda, do you know how many anonymous complaints I received when I first started as Superintendent?" Shawn tried to reassure her. "All because we don't fit the mold. It means you're doing your job right, Wanda."

"I suppose so..." Wanda said, unconvinced still that she was doing a good enough job to keep her position as Principal.

Shawn, sensing the doubt that was plaguing Wanda's voice and mind, continued. "We'll sort this out. Do you know anyone who would have any issues with you?"

Wanda leaned back in her chair and stroked her chin. As she reflected on her interactions with the students, she realized that none of them, except for the wrestler who had knocked her down previously, would file an anonymous complaint about her. Then her mind wandered to the faculty, and she instantly thought of Coach. He had been harsh towards her in the beginning, but Wanda truly felt like he was coming around to her.

She thought harder and finally asked, "How many were there?"

"Three," Shawn said curiously.

"And when did they start?" Wanda asked with suspicions running rampant in her mind.

"About a month ago," Shawn said. "Why?"

That would have been around the same time Robert and she had gotten into the heated discussion in front of Jesus, Quentin, and Mike. Could Robert have been so upset over Wanda punishing those boys that he would retaliate like that? He wouldn't, would he?

"Wanda?" Shawn asked, snapping Wanda out of her train of thought.

"Sorry, Shawn, I was just thinking of who it could have been that filed these complaints."

"Any ideas?"

Wanda paused before she answered as she contemplated what to say next. She wasn't sure if she should be honest about her suspicions with Shawn or keep them to herself until she had proof that it was Robert, assuming that's who it was.

"None. Everyone at the school seems to respect me," Wanda confessed. "The *only* one I could even think of it possibly being was Coach because he's been hostile towards me in the past, but over the last month, he's become a lot less hostile and more friendly."

"By Coach, you mean Peter Dirdick?"

"Yes, that's him," Wanda confirmed. "But I really don't think it's him, Sir."

"Wanda," Shawn started while he clicked his tongue. "Sometimes the ones closest to us are the ones who betray us quickest. What's that saying?"

"Keep your friends close and your enemies closer," Wanda mumbled her words as realization sank in. Maybe it hadn't been Robert. After all, since the smoking incident, she hadn't had any run-ins with him like that. Robert could have simply been having a bad day that day.

George brought Wanda a glass of cold sweet tea, noticing that something was plaguing her already troubled mind. He had seen his wife going through a lot of trials and tribulations this school year and he was worried about her. He wasn't sure how long she could take the stress and hate before she succumbed to it and let it eat her alive.

Wanda glanced over at George and smiled weakly at him. She took the glass from his hands and brought it to her lips. After a few sips of the tea, she turned to look at George. "Someone filed anonymous complaints against me to the District Office," Wanda finally confessed to her husband.

George raised an eyebrow and scrunched up his nose. "Fo' what?"

"They didn't really say." Wanda let out a defeated sigh. "It was more of a complaint on the way I was running the school. All the letters pretty much said were, 'She's running that school into the ground. Fire her!'"

George blinked a few times and scoffed. "Why, tha' ain't right by no means. Yousa doin' a might' fine job of runnin' tha' school, hunny."

"I don't know, George." Wanda paused and looked deep into her husband's eyes. "Am I cut out for this job? The situation with Coach at the beginning of the year, the deal with Robert last month, and now anonymous complaints? Not to mention the way it is affecting Michelle."

George held a hand up and leaned on his knees to look deeper into his wife's eyes. "'Chelle thinks the worl'o'ya." George corrected her. "'Er Mama is 'er biggest 'ero. She looks uptaya."

Wanda bit her lip and directed her gaze away from the captivating look her husband was giving her. She didn't want to give in to him. For once, she desired a moment to indulge in self-pity. She was tired of always having to be so strong.

"I don't know if I want to do this next year, George." Wanda chewed on her lip and looked back at George.

"'Cha mean?" George asked as he tilted his head to the side.

"I don't know if I want to be the principal next year," she began. "Maybe I should just go back to teaching. Teaching was my passion, and the students loved me."

"You don' think the stud'nts love ya now?" George asked out of genuine curiosity. Out of everything she complained about at the end of her workdays, it was never the students. Staff and faculty? Sure, a couple of times. Students? Never.

Wanda frowned at the point her husband was making. "No, most of them seem to respect me," she admitted.

"But the public doesn't, and neither does the staff or faculty."

"Hon', you'ra basin' this all on t'ree peo'le."

Wanda looked away, ashamed that she was making this all about her, truly over three people. "George, it just doesn't feel fair that I'm going through this. I have been nothing but caring for these students my entire career. I love them like I love Michelle."

George wrapped his arm around the love of his life and pulled her in closer. "Lis'n me, Wanda. You is one the bes' damn thin's to happen to Holcom' Schools. You got inta education fo' one reason an' one reason only. To help them studen's."

Suddenly, a crash came from the sunroom. George and Wanda both jumped out of their respective recliners in their den and ran to their sunroom. A brick-sized hole stained the otherwise pristine glass window. On the ground, worshiped by thousands of shards of glass, sat a brick with a note tied to it.

Wanda slowly walked to the brick and leaned down to pick it up. She slipped the perfectly folded white slip of paper from between the brown twine and red brick they tucked it between. Slowly, she unfolded the piece of paper to reveal a note that read: *Get out of town, bitch!*

A tear slipped out of Wanda's eye and streamed down her face. Her worst fears had come true. She was afraid for her life because of her position. Being pushed out of her home because of this job was the last thing she wanted, but here she was facing yet another obstacle in her way.

Another tear rolled down the opposite side of her cheek as the thoughts of death and anger swarmed through her mind. She trembled as she let her hands fall to her side as she shook. The paper fell from her hand and floated gracefully to the ground. Wanda bent down with shaky knees to pick up the paper.

George walked up behind Wanda and placed his hand gently on her sobbing shoulder. He looked over her shoulder, down at the letter. Feeling the rage building up in his now reddened face, he glanced back up and out the window. In the distance, he caught the glare of a pickup truck's taillights leaving his driveway and out to the dirt road.

"We'll take the brick and run it for prints," the Sheriff, Frederick Grant, said while he stroked his white mustache. "But I can't guarantee we'll find anything. Especially since hands were all over it gloveless. *Ahem*."

Wanda's face went red with embarrassment as she glanced over at George. "Tha's-a my fault, Chief," George said, glancing away from his wife and looking back at Frederick. "I can tell ya, tha's-a late model 1980's pickup truck yer look'n for."

Frederick raised an eyebrow and glanced at George. "You sure?"

"Hundred'cent. I know the tail'ights ofa new ef-fone-fitty any day."

The chief nodded. "Understood, George." He got back into his car and rolled down the window. "Wanda?"

"Yes, Chief?"

"For what it's worth, I think you're the best damn thing that's happened to our school district." He nodded his head and rolled up his window before taking off down the driveway and out to the dirt road.

Wanda held back a tear as she leaned into her husband. Luckily, Michelle was at her grandparents' house and didn't have to experience the night's horrors. But what if she had been home? This kind of thing could have traumatized her. She could have been playing in the sunroom and been scarred by glass shards or hit with the brick.

How could someone be so cruel as to put a family at risk? To put a child in harm's way? Was it worth fighting for this job when her family's safety was in jeopardy? Part of her felt selfish and guilty for ever taking the job and putting her family in that position in the first place.

"George?" she squeaked.

"Yess'on?" George said as he looked down at his tiny wife. Her slight frame appeared delicate, but her resilience was amazing.

"I think I've made a decision on what I want to do."

George's eyebrows met his hairline as his eyes went wide. "Wha's 'at?"

"I want to keep being the best damn thing that's ever happened to Holcomb County Schools."

Chapter 9

School Board

A few days after Wanda and George's home had a brick thrown through it, Wanda was sitting at her desk back at East Holcomb High. She couldn't focus after the events that had transpired on Friday. Not only had she faced anonymous complaints, but she was also now facing threats on her and her family's well-being.

Her phone rang, and she glanced across her desk at the phone screen. She sighed as she saw the number for the District Office ring across her phone. The phone continued to ring as Wanda put her head in her hands. She reached over and picked up the phone receiver.

"Wanda," she answered. She was expecting the worst from this phone call.

"Wanda," Shawn Carlile started, as he cleared his throat. "I heard about what happened at your home over the weekend, and I have to say I'm sorry to hear about it."

"Thank you, Shawn," Wanda said, waiting for Shawn to get to the point of the phone call. She knew condolences weren't the only reason she was getting a call from the Superintendent.

"The School Board wants to have a performance review," Shawn finally said after an awkward silence. "The School Board has voted to create this new policy." "For all the principals?" Wanda asked as she leaned back.

"No," Shawn said as he coughed. "Just for the new ones."

"Shawn," Wanda snarled. "I am the *only* new principal in the district. This has never been done before. Why am I just now hearing about this policy change?"

"I know, Wanda," Shawn returned with a slight sigh. "I know. Personnel matters are considered executive privilege, and are confidential for legal reasons. I wasn't at liberty to say. However, we received another complaint this morning that was sent directly to the Board members. This one, I couldn't avoid."

"What is so serious that it has their attention?" Wanda questioned, a bit of hostility entering her voice.

An uncomfortable silence lingered before Shawn finally spoke back up. "They don't feel like their kids are safe around you after the events of the weekend. We live in a small town, Wanda, word spreads like wildfire. They are concerned that the violence against you will intensify and extend to the school. There's genuine concern about someone causing you serious harm."

"The events of the weekend?" Wanda scoffed. "So, because some ignorant, arrogant person decided to threaten *my* family, all of a sudden I'm not qualified to be the principal of a school? All of a sudden they're worried about me getting hurt? Why have none of the School Board members called me themselves to express their genuine concern for my safety?"

"Nobody in power is *saying* you aren't qualified for the job, Wanda..." Shawn began.

"You're right, nobody is saying it because they can't with a good conscience, say something they know to be untrue. Anonymous threats, bricks thrown through my window. The only ones saying it are the cowards behind closed doors, and that should tell you all you need to know."

"I know that, Wanda."

"Do you, Shawn?" Wanda snapped as she slammed her hand down on the desk and brought the receiver closer to her mouth. "Because you seem to be taking *their* side in all of this. I took this job because I thought you would have my back, I thought I had someone who believed in me in the Administration. What happened to the man who gave me my first job all those years ago, Shawn?"

Shawn cleared his throat awkwardly as he contemplated what Wanda was saying. "I'm trying," he finally whispered. "I'm walking a fine line here, Wanda. I have a family, a wife, kids, who I have to feed, too. They've threatened to come after me if we can't get this situation under control. If you get injured on the job again or someone threatens the school, the Board will come after me and take both of us down. You really think I want to admit defeat? You think I want to give up on my first hire as a Principal *and* as a Superintendent? Admit that I was wrong? It's that, or be fired and have someone come in who will force you out, Wanda. I'm still fighting for you. Please don't get that twisted."

Wanda's breath slowed as she sat back in her chair. She shook her head and inhaled deeply. As she exhaled, she said, "I'm sorry, Shawn. I know you're trying. I just feel like I'm fighting a losing battle."

"No battle is a losing battle for people like us, Wanda," Shawn assured.

"Then why does it feel like no matter how many steps forward I take; I get pushed back two more?"

Shawn chuckled and Wanda wrinkled her nose. "You're fighting an uphill battle, not a losing one."

Wanda sighed. "What's the difference, Shawn? Either way, I can't win for losing."

"Where's the woman I hired as a teacher ten years ago?" Shawn countered. Wanda winced as she felt the sting of her words being used against her. "The one whose resilience never let even the worst of adversities keep her down?" Wanda was silent. "She believed she didn't need to cross those mountains you're facing now, because you could simply *move* them out of the way with your strength, Wanda."

Wanda chewed on her bottom lip and slumped back in her chair. "How?"

"How what?"

"How do I win them over, Shawn?" Wanda asked, nearly pleading for his help and guidance. "I need to know how you did it. I need your strength."

"By being Wanda Hare. By being the best damn thing that's ever happened to Holcomb County Schools."

Wanda sat timidly in the back room of the board meeting. She awaited the Board members to re-enter the room. They'd taken a brief recess before going into their special meeting's Executive Session. Wanda was nervous, to say the least. This could be the moment that made or broke her career.

The door opened and Shawn stepped in. "How are you doing, Wanda?" Shawn asked. "Board is almost back in."

"I'm scared for my life, Shawn." Wanda closed her eyes and leaned her head back against the wall. "This could ruin my career. Teaching is all I have ever cared about."

Shawn sat down next to Wanda and placed a hand on her shoulder. "Wanda, just go in there and be yourself. Show them the Wanda Hare that I hired ten years ago. Prove to them you're fit for the job."

She nodded and the door opened. The district's solicitor entered, giving Wanda and Shawn a once-over before sticking his nose up in the air. He walked to his seat at the end of the Board's table and sat down, pulling out a pen and paper.

The solicitor was followed by the Board members. The first to enter was Henry Thorne, President of the Board. Following him was Vice President Craig Greene and then Gene Young, Secretary. The three of them entered, chatting amongst themselves, and ignoring Wanda and Shawn. Finally, the remaining two Board members, Brad Manning and the newest Board member, Terry Teether, entered.

Terry stopped and turned to Shawn and Wanda. With a smile, he said, "Hello Shawn. Hello Wanda. I hope you both are doing well."

The kindness in Terry's eyes and voice was genuine, of that Wanda was sure. She smiled back and nodded at Terry. "I'm doing well, Mr. Teether. I hope you are also."

"Mr. Teether," President Thorne called out. "Please take your seat so we can begin the Principal's review."

Terry nodded at Wanda and Shawn and departed for his seat. "Teether is our best hope," Shawn whispered to Wanda, who silently nodded.

"Wanda," President Thorne began. "You have received several complaints over the last several months in your tenure as Principal at East Holcomb High School."

Wanda winced at the words. She knew about the complaints, but it didn't make it easier to stomach. The complaints stung, because she had always prided herself in making a difference in the lives of the students. Complaints like the ones she had received made her feel like she would never accomplish that again.

"Mr. President," Wanda began. "I don't believe these complaints are fair."

"Would you care to explain, Mrs. Hare?" Craig Greene, asked.

"None of them have been signed," she said. "I don't think they can truly be trusted."

"Just because an anonymous member of the community doesn't want to face backlash for their opinion," Gene Young started as he leaned forward on his elbows. "Does not make the complaints any less valid."

"I understand," Wanda said and looked down at her feet. When she looked up, she was smiling. After reaching into her briefcase and pulling out a stack of papers, she distributed copies of them to each of the Board members. She carefully stacked three pieces of paper in front of each Board member. They all glared at her, except Terry who smiled and responded with a quiet thank you.

"If you'll direct your attention to the first page," Wanda began. "You'll see that our attendance record is the highest it has been in ten years. More students are feeling the Panther pride with a 15% increase in attendance records and 20% increase at sporting events. We also have more students who are participating in extracurriculars."

The Board studied the papers in front of them. Scowls crossed their faces. "What about discipline, Mrs. Hare?" Brad Manning asked, pausing on the second page. A smile crossed his face for a split second before disappearing into a more poker face.

"I'm glad you asked, Mr. Manning," Wanda smiled as she spoke the words. "The second page will show that our disciplinary incidents are at a record low. Not just for our school's history, but that of the entire school district."

Terry, shuffling to the third page after reviewing the first, smiled and looked up. "Mrs. Hare, would you please move on to the last page?"

"Of course, Mr. Teether." Wanda shuffled her papers and held up the last paper to face the Board and solicitor. "Gentlemen, as you can see on the last page, our school has seen some of the highest grade averages in our school's history. I predict that will only increase during the second half of the year."

"Mrs. Hare," Henry huffed. "To be honest, this does little to change my mind. This is all fine and dandy, but the safety of our students is more important than these cherry picked statistics."

"I don't know," Terry spoke up as he leaned back in his seat. "My daughter feels pretty safe at school. She is even excited about school since Mrs. Hare took over this year."

"Mr. Teether," The President spoke. "Your daughter does not speak for the majority of the school."

"Neither do anonymous complaints and a physical attack on a district Principal."

President Thorne slammed his fist into the desk, causing Wanda to wince. "I will not have these things dismissed, Mr. Teether."

Shawn stood up and walked to Wanda, motioning with his head for her to sit back down. "Mr. President,"

Shawn said after he cleared his throat and gathered the board's attention. "If I may."

"Go ahead, Mr. Carlile," President Thorne said.

"Thank you," Shawn smiled and nodded at him. "I would like to propose a public hearing."

"Public hearing? I think this needs to be figured out tonight." President Thorne scowled at Shawn.

"After the evening news covered Mrs. Hare's hiring at the beginning of the school year," Shawn started as the Board listened intently. "They would be all over her firing. It would not be a good look to give the public, or to your constituents. They should have a chance to have their voices heard. And anyone with complaints can also be heard at that time."

"I'll make the motion," Terry spoke up.

Suddenly, a wicked grin made its way across President Thorne's face. "If the Board insists on prancing Mrs. Hare out there for a dog and pony show, then so be it. I will second the motion."

The other three Board members were stunned, but looked over at the President. They saw his smile and reluctantly voted in favor, following with all yays to indicate their vote. "Then the motion passes," President Thorne said with a devious smile. "Mrs. Hare, you are to report to the Board meeting tomorrow evening for a public performance review. The public will be allowed to comment, if they so choose. You and Mr. Carlile are excused so that we may conclude our discussion of executive matters."

When Shawn and Wanda closed the door behind them, Wanda asked, "What were you thinking? I could barely hold my composure here, much less in front of the public."

Shawn looked over at Wanda. "You've spoken in front of crowds larger than this, in front of opposing teams who wanted to destroy our school's team. You always find a way to speak the right words at the right time."

"Why a public meeting?" Wanda asked, confused.

"To show them – and you – that you have more support than they think you do."

Wanda sat with her legs crossed in the board room with her gray pencil skirt, waiting for the School Board to call for the public comment section of the meeting to commence. The President finished up his spiel about investing in sports to offset the rising cost of inflation, and finally said, "We will now entertain comments from the public about school district matters. Every person gets three minutes of time, and please state your name as you begin." Shawn stood and walked to the podium.

"Thank you, Mr. President," he started, as he looked at each of the Board members. If one didn't know any better, one would have assumed that most of the Board Members were related. White men in their late sixties and early seventies with grey hair and clean-shaven faces, a true moniker of the times. Most of them had dark brown eyes that seemed to suck the soul out of everyone they locked eyes with, except Terry Teething, who had soothing blue eyes which seemed to hold a tempest of solitude, perhaps even one of peace and harmony. In fact, he stood out as the only one who wouldn't be guessed as related to the crew of elderly white men. He was younger, probably in his early for-ties. Something about his aura stood out from the rest, almost like he was the yin to their yang. "Shawn Carlile, gentlemen. Superintendent of the Holcomb County School District."

"You may proceed, Mr. Carlile," said President Thorne.

Wanda rolled her eyes at how diplomatic Shawn was being, standing there with his bright smile. She knew he had to put on a certain facade to fool the white hairs, but it didn't make her any less disgusted to know this dog and pony show was all about putting her on display. "Mrs. Wanda Hare is our only new Principal this year. Wanda. I hired Wanda as a teacher ten years ago because of her tenacity and dedication to the profession. When I took the job as Superintendent of Holcomb County

Schools, I knew she was the one ready to take the reins on East Holcomb." Shawn looked at her and nodded his head toward the podium.

Inhaling deeply, Wanda allowed the cool air of the board room to fill her lungs before exhaling warmth into the room's coolness. She stood and made her way to the podium, cautiously glancing around the room. She brushed the sides of her skirt and leaned into the microphone. "Thank you, Board members, for having me tonight. I look forward to your review of my performance." *And to make my case against whatever you are thinking.*

The President of the Board, Henry Thorne, squinted his eyes at Wanda. "Wanda," he began as he adjusted his microphone. He sat up straight in his chair and continued, "We have had several complaints about you since you began as the Principal of East Holcomb High. Can you explain them to us? This is troublesome to hear, if I am being honest."

"Mr. President, I would first like to say that the complaints are baseless. The most recent issue was about an *actual physical attack* on my family. It has nothing to do with my job as Principal at East Holcomb."

"What happens when the violence seeps into the school, Wanda?" Another board member, Craig Greene, spat back.

"I do not believe that we have to fear that. The complaints have been anonymous, cowards hidden behind closed doors ashamed to make their position publicly known. If these complaints and threats were valid, we would have already seen it spilling into the school. However, if violence occurs on the school grounds, we have an excellent Security Officer in Mr. Cooke, who will protect our students."

"And you? Will he also protect you?" A third member, Gene Young, asked as he leaned forward on his elbows and cocked his head to the side. "I recall an incident from last semester where you had a fight with a student and ended up in the hospital with staples in your head."

"I believe he will." Silence followed Wanda's statement as the Board looked at one another - all except the junior member, Terry Teether. His focus remained on Wanda. His look was more one of admiration than admonition and he continued. "I believe you are mistaken about the incident, however. There were two students fighting. I was the closest adult in authority, and I had to make a move before a student was hurt. The students, as the Board will surely recognize, are my first priority."

As President Thorne opened his mouth to speak, Terry leaned into the microphone and spoke up. "Mrs. Hare," he began. President Thorne glared at Terry as he closed his mouth. "Please tell us why you are so adamant about keeping your position as Principal?"

"Maybe explain why you should remain employed by the Holcomb County School District, Wanda," Gene added. "Because as of right now, your performance is suspect, at best. We must make a decision that is going to best benefit our school district and ensure the safety and well-being of our students. I don't feel like you are the one who should hold the position of Principal at this time."

Wanda's heart began beating out of her chest. She closed her eyes and took a deep breath. When she opened her eyes, she had a look of dedication in her eyes. She was determined to prove to this Board why she should keep her job. "I stand before you today, not just as the first female Principal in Holcomb County, but as one of you. I am a part of this community; I am a product of this district and these classrooms. We have faced many challenges together, but look at us now. We have transformed, we have grown, and we have prevailed.

"When I started my journey here, many doubted. They doubted a woman's ability to lead, to shape, to inspire. But I saw a different picture. I saw promise. I saw potential. I saw the future of these children, our children, gleaming with possibilities. They are the reason I am here. They are the reason I fight." Wanda paused and looked around at the board.

Every Board member was leaning forward, propped up on their elbows, with their attention intently gazed on Wanda. Scowls filled most of their faces, all except Terry. Terry leaned back in his chair and smiled. Wanda made eye contact with him and they locked eyes.

Terry smiled and nodded at her, giving her his seal of approval at the way she was carrying herself.

"Our school now holds the highest mid-year progress report grade ever in the school's history," Wanda continued with pride. She held up a copy of the report card that she had finished earlier that day. As she made her way to the dais and began handing out copies of the report she had poured hours of sweat and tears into, she continued speaking. "This is not my achievement alone, but ours. Yours. Together, we have defied the odds. Together, we have proven that when you believe in a dream, when you work towards it with all your heart, miracles do happen." Wanda returned to the podium and looked down at the report card. The school's average grade was a B, the highest in all the school District and the highest ever for East Holcomb. Their mid-year test scores were marks above what they had been in years past, greatly surpassing their highest marks in the school's history.

She looked back up at the board and smiled. "I've been tested, challenged, and criticized," she said. "But I stood firm because this is not just a job for me. This is my life's mission. I am here to make a difference, to make a change. And my resolve only grows stronger with each passing day."

Wanda took in a deep breath and turned to face the standing room only crowd that she had been avoiding. She scanned the room. She saw Robert standing against a wall in the back corner of the board room. She couldn't get a read of support for her or the Board on his face. Looking over the rest of the crowd, she spotted Craig and Katherine sitting beside each other with worry stricken across their faces. Beside them was Mike, which surprised her the most of the three. And finally, her eyes met the brown eyes of the reason she was fighting - Michelle. She looked up at George and smiled as he placed his hand on Michelle's shoulder.

"Remember this," she started as she glanced across the crowd. Anxious ears listened as she spoke. Angry glares turned to curious stares while the compassionate melted in their seats with admiration. "Our children are watching us. My daughter, your daughters, our sons, they are observing us. They are learning from us. My daughter was elated when she found out that I was becoming Principal. She saw my dreams being realized. And I want her, and all our children, to know that they can achieve their dreams too, regardless of their gender.

"Let us not forget, we are the role models. We are the ones they look up to. We have the power to break stereotypes, to shatter glass ceilings, to rewrite the rules."

Wanda turned back to face the Board. "I am not just the first female principal in the Holcomb County School District, I am a symbol of hope. A beacon of change. A testament of what women can achieve when given the opportunity. I am proof that dreams do come true.

"So, let us keep dreaming. Let's keep striving. Let's keep pushing boundaries. Because our children deserve nothing less. They deserve a future filled with opportunities. They deserve to see that their dreams are valid and achievable."

Wanda paused. She looked at each one of the Board members. She landed on Gene. "Despite everything, I will keep going. I will keep fighting. I will keep making East Holcomb High a home for dreams, a beacon of hope, a place where futures are shaped. For East Holcomb High, for Holcomb County Schools, for our children, and for all the dreams yet to come true." Wanda's bottom lip quivered as she came to the end of her speech.

An eerie silence filled the room as the tension thickened the air around Wanda. A clap broke through the silence, instantly dismantling the tension that had been building up in the room. Another clap followed, then another, and another, and another. Within a few seconds, over half the audience was clapping and standing up to support Wanda.

President Thorne began beating his gavel on the dais and shouted, "Order! Everyone sit down. There will be order in this Board room." The thunderous outpour of love drowned out the chairman's demands as they continued with the beat of their own drum.

Wanda turned and looked back at Michelle, smiling as she clapped along with the crowd. George looked at Wanda through the rims of his glasses and nodded at her. Wanda smiled and closed her eyes, taking in a deep breath as she turned back around.

The applause slowly came to an end, fading away into the anger that fueled President Thorne. With reddened cheeks and steam bellowing from his ears, he glanced out across the crowd before his gaze finally settled on Wanda, who remained calm, cool, and collected as she took a deep breath, awaiting the Board's next move.

Craig cleared his throat and leaned into the microphone. "Mrs. Hare, you have made an interesting case for you to keep your position. As the Vice President of this Board, I would like to call a motion that we allow Wanda Hare to keep her position as Principal of East Holcomb High School through the end of the current school year, at which point we will revisit the final results from the school's year-end report card as well as monitoring the safety of our students." Gasps came from some members of the audience as they, despite Wanda's compelling speech, still expected the Board to fire and replace her tonight. Murmurs from dissatisfied crowd members erupted.

"Mr. President," Terry began as he leaned into his microphone. "If you are going to demand order in the board room during an outburst of support from the crowd, then I expect you to hold dissenters to the same standards. Please call for order in the room at once." The President, however, didn't have to call for decorum as the room came to a quiet standstill at Terry's blunt words. "I second Mr. Greene's motion."

Henry Thorne clenched his jaw as he ground his teeth together. He exhaled loudly and unclenched his jaw, leaning into the microphone. With venom dripping from his voice, he said, "There is a motion on the floor that Mrs. Wanda Hare keeps her position as Principal of East Holcomb High School through the end of the year, understanding that we will review her performance again at that time." Henry took in a deep breath and as he exhaled, he said, "My vote is Nay. Mr. Greene?"

"Yay," Craig said as stunned gasps came from the crowd. "Mrs. Hare has proven herself, both with her speech here tonight and through the results of the progress reports, that she is more than capable of handling this job."

"Mr. Young?" The President asked, looking over at Gene.

"Nay," Gene stated as he stared deep into Wanda's eyes, like a succubus stealing the soul of its victim. Wanda stood steadfast, never wavering at Gene's gaze. Despite being down two votes to one, she was confident that she had done enough to sway the Board's decision. "Our students are not safe in the school as long as Wanda is in charge of the school. We cannot risk the safety of our students just to prove a woman can do this job. If that was the case, why not hire a monkey to prove a point?" There were chuckles from the dissenters in the crowd, and Henry smiled.

"Mr. Teether?" Henry slowly turned his head to look at Terry and squinted his eyes, already anticipating the yay from Terry.

"Yay." Terry said as the crowd hissed at his answer. "I have three daughters at home who have all been inspired by Mrs. Hare and the way she has handled herself in the position. My daughters, our daughters, will all look up to Mrs. Hare as a trailblazer, as someone who proved that women are capable of the same achievement men are. Mr. Young, in response to your comments, maybe we should replace some of our Board members with monkeys. It would still be a circus up here, but they may be able to do a better job of keeping hate and bigotry out of these meetings." Most of the crowd laughed, while some booed.

Gene's eyes went wide, and his cheeks lit up on fire as he slammed his fist against the dais. The crowd quieted as his outburst began, "Mr. Teether, I demand respect as a member of this Board of Education from the rest of the Board members, despite our difference in opinions. I *will* move to have you removed if you insult a board member again."

Terry laughed out loud at Gene's fruitless threat. "And if you disrespect Mrs. Hare again by comparing her to a monkey or refusing to address her like you do her male counterparts, as Mrs. Hare, then I will move to have *you* removed from the Board." The crowd stood and cheered for Terry's defense of Wanda.

Henry banged his gavel on the dais again. "Order in the board room, I demand! Order!" The crowd quieted down and sat back in their seats. Henry cleared his throat as the crowd quieted and looked from Board member to Board member until his eyes landed on the man at the very end. The man who had been quiet from the beginning of the proceedings until now, Brad Manning, sat silently, waiting for his turn to vote.

"Currently, we have a two yays and two nays for the motion on the floor. We have one last Board member to vote. Mr. Manning," Henry smiled at Brad, knowing that Brad was also against Wanda from prior conversations. "Do you vote yay or nay for the motion to keep Wanda Hare as the Principal of East Holcomb High School through the end of the school year, at which time we will review her performance and the safety of her students?"

Brad sat back, twiddling his thumbs together as his eyes glanced up at the ceiling. He glanced back down at Wanda, still patiently standing, awaiting her final judgement. "Coming into this meeting, I was ready to replace Mrs. Hare with her Assistant Principal, Mr. Kane," Brad confessed. "Due to recent incidents and anonymous complaints, I felt our students weren't receiving the education quality we expect or feeling safe on school grounds." Wanda looked down as she fought back tears, expecting this to be another nay and the next vote to be to replace her.

Michelle, not quite sure what was going on, tugged on her dad's denim coveralls. He looked down at her and brought a finger to his lips. He smiled a reassuring smile at her. How he could smile at such a tough time was beyond Michelle, but she trusted her Dad and that was enough for her to smile as she looked back at her Mom.

Wanda lifted her head up and opened her mouth to defend herself, but Brad continued into the microphone before she could get a word out. "However," he began, looking from Wanda to Gene and Henry. "After hearing Mrs. Hare speak and seeing the results of the school's mid-year report card, I see I was sadly mistaken."

Wanda's eyes went wide as her heartbeat quickened. Brad looked back at Wanda's changed expression sprawled across her face and smiled at her with a nod. "Mrs. Hare has earned the chance to finish out the school year. Our students are thriving underneath her leadership, and we would be doing a disservice to ourselves and our students if we were to relieve Mrs. Hare of her duties. My vote is yay."

The crowd erupted in a cheer as most of the people in the room stood up, clapped, shouted, and whistled. Amidst the applause and cheering, the President's gavel was drowned out, concealing the sound of wood banging against wood. President Thorne attempted to shout out over the crowd, but to no avail. He sighed and sat back in his seat, hanging his head in defeat.

As the deafening cheers and applause toned down, Henry looked up and over the crowd. His gaze changed to Shawn Carlile, who was smiling brightly at the results of the vote. Henry looked back at the rest of the board, a scowl across his fellow dissenters' faces and smiles across those who had voted yay for Wanda. Finally, his eyes landed on Wanda. Stoic, she stood there awaiting the Board's next step.

"Mrs. Hare," Henry said as he cleared his throat. "We have granted you a continuance of your position as Principal of East Holcomb High School. However, do not think you are off the hook just yet. We will be watching, grading, and monitoring your performance and the safety of our students with a fine-tooth comb. Any slip ups, any mistakes, we will see. Be your best, Mrs. Hare, for this could be your last chance."

Chapter 10

Therapy

"**M**rs. Wanda!" Katherine shouted as she entered Wanda's office beside Craig. Katherine was dragging Craig by the hand as Wanda looked up from the report she had been working on. "*Please* tell Craig there is nothing wrong with men exploring their feelings."

Wanda smiled at the two students. Since the day they had both come to visit her in the hospital, Wanda had always believed they could make a good couple. Not just in the way they look, but in their very souls and who they were as people. They seemed to click on every level, and the way Katherine held on to Craig's hand was certainly a sign that she felt the same way.

"Craig," Wanda started as she leaned back in her chair and crossed her legs. She smoothed the flat of her skirt and cleared her throat. "Men are just as much allowed to feel and express emotion as women are. Now what has brought this on?"

"Welllll," Katherine started, rolling her eyes and looking over at Craig. "This one has been acting off for the last few weeks. And he won't tell me why!" She pouted her lips out and turned back to face Wanda. "Make him tell me why he's acting weird, Mrs. Wanda!"

Wanda chuckled and leaned forward, propping herself up on her elbows as she looked at Katherine. "Katherine," Wanda started, stifling a giggle. She had a feeling she and Katherine both knew why Craig was acting strange around her, but she didn't want to be the one to say it. "Just as it is okay for Craig to have feelings, he isn't obligated to tell anybody those feelings."

Katherine moved around to the chair in front of Wanda's desk and slumped down in it. "Well, it would be healthier for him if he opened up to somebody!"

"Just because he won't open up to you," Wanda leaned back and crossed her arms. "Doesn't mean he won't open up to anybody." Katherine's face lit up like a brand-new lightbulb as an idea went off in her head.

Wanda's eyebrows turned in and her face scrunched up as she waited for the reason Katherine had suddenly become so joyous.

Katherine stood up and walked to Craig. She led him by the hand to the chair she had been slumped in seconds ago and pointed towards it. "Sit."

Craig raised an eyebrow as he looked from her bright and bubbly face to Wanda's smirk she wore at the way the two of them interacted. He finally looked back at Katherine and said, "Why?"

"Just sit," Katherine whined.

Craig let out a large huff and took his turn to slump into the chair. He looked at Wanda and she still wore a smirk across her lips. Her gaze was at Katherine, waiting for her to reveal her grand plan. "I'm sitting," Craig moaned. "Now what, your Majesty?"

For a brief moment, Wanda saw a hint of red blush flow across Katherine's cheeks. It was only for a moment, for she immediately turned back to the bright lightbulb and spilled her plan. "You said he *should* talk to someone, right?" Katherine asked.

Wanda held her pointer finger up and leaned forward. "Now, I don't think that is what I said."

"Semantics," Katherine waved her off and smiled widely. "He *should* talk to someone about his feelings, and there is literally no better person than Mrs. Hare."

"Katherine," Wanda started, muffling a laugh. "That is Craig's choice.""I *would* like a say in my own decisions, Katherine." Craig grunted and crossed his arms.

"Too bad, decision made, byyyyye," Katherine said as she skipped out of the office and closed the door behind her.

"Craig," Wanda started as her eyebrows relaxed and her cheek muscles loosened. "If you aren't comfortable..."

"I think I love her, Mrs. Hare," Craig blurted out, almost leaping out of his chair from the force of him leaning forward. Wanda's eyes went big, a reaction she did not mean to expel. "I know, I know, love is a strong word. But..." Craig sat back in his seat and hung his head down.

Wanda scrunched her nose and tilted her head slightly to the side. "But what, Craig?"

"But I don't know how to tell her, I don't know if she feels the same way, I don't even know if she would even consider dating me, much less loving me like I love her."

Wanda's face relaxed and a pencil thin smile wrote its way on her face. "Craig, I wouldn't start with the whole love thing. Take it step-by-step. Tell her you like her, give it a shot."

"What if she doesn't feel the same way?" He looked up, his eyes glistening with fear.

"You've never been rejected before, have you Craig?"

Craig went wide eyed at Wanda's question. He sat up in his chair and pondered the question. "Not by girls. Or sports. Or friends. Or anything, really."

"Have you ever been afraid of rejection before?"

"No, not really," he answered while glancing away from Wanda.

Wanda smiled. "You're not afraid of rejection, you're afraid of falling in love."

"Falling?" He chuckled slightly and looked back up at Wanda. "I've already fallen. I'm afraid of getting back up and seeing who noticed."

"I think the one person you truly should care about seeing you fall in love, already knows you're on that journey," Wanda said with a bright smile and a wink at Craig.

His eyes went wide, and he stood up. "You think she already knows?!"

"I don't have any confirmation, but I have a pretty good inkling of it." Wanda stood up and walked around the desk. She placed a hand on Craig's shoulder and leaned in. "I think she likes you, Craig," Wanda whispered. As the sound of the bell rang, she led Craig to the door and opened it. When she opened it, Katherine fell forward and into Craig's arms. Craig reached out and pulled her in to avoid dropping her on the ground.

"Were you listening to our conversation?" Craig asked in an accusatory tone as he scrunched his nose and furrowed his eyebrows. His face was beet red from the potential embarrassment he faced in revealing his emotions to the one girl he had ever felt this way for.

"Well, not exactly," Katherine said as she stood back up and brushed herself off. The only thing she couldn't brush off was the bright pink blush that had reddened her face after she fell into Craig's arms. "I couldn't hear anything through the door," she muttered.

Wanda laughed and shooed her hand at the two love-birds. "Alright, you two, get to class before you're late."

"Yes, Mrs. Hare," they said in unison.

Later in the week, Wanda was strolling the halls of East Holcomb High when she passed the boy's bathroom where she had caught Mike, Quentin, and Jesus smoking. As she made her way back to her office, she couldn't help but to think about Mike. Although she thought he would be the honest one, his response to being caught and questioned about smoking was unlike him.

Mike Kramer had been an honors student until three and a half years ago when his parents divorced. She remembered he confided in her during their English class, explaining that he would have to step back from the honors program because of falling behind. It truly broke Wanda's heart when he told her because he was one of the brightest freshmen in the school.

Following his parents' divorce, he began to struggle with schoolwork when he transitioned from honors to intermediate classes. The main reason, Wanda believed, that he was doing so poorly in school was because he spent so much time in detention these last two years. All that time in detention had resulted in him not being in class enough to learn the material. Wanda frowned as she unlocked her office door and walked in.

"Mrs. Hare?" Wanda heard an eerily familiar voice call.

Wanda turned around and saw the face of the student she had just been thinking about. "Mike," Wanda started, turning her head slightly to the side and raising her eyebrows. "Are you okay?" Wanda could see a hint of blue outlining his eye through the stringy black hair that was covering it. She took a step forward and squinted. "Did you get into a fight?"

He shook his head and brushed his hair to further cover his eye. "No, Ma'am." "No, you aren't okay or no, you didn't get in a fight?" Wanda asked, hoping it was the latter.

Mike nibbled at his swollen lip and looked away from Wanda's caring gaze. "Both."

Wanda stifled a gasp as she stepped back and held the door open for Mike. She waved her arm towards her office. "Come in," she said. "Sit down and let's talk."

Mike looked up at her. In the eye not covered by his hair, Wanda could have sworn she saw the glistening of a tear threatening to escape. Mike nodded and walked swiftly past her before sitting in a seat in front of Wanda's desk. Wanda followed behind him and made her way to her side of the desk, taking a seat in her chair.

The two sat in silence for several minutes before Mike would ever make eye contact with Wanda. His eyes buzzed around the room, looking everywhere but into Wanda's gaze as if she were Medusa herself. Once his eyes finally landed like a fly on Wanda, he broke and tears flowed from his eyes, down his cheeks, and soaked the front of his shirt. "You know my parents divorced a few years ago, right?" he finally asked.

"Yes, I remember you telling me about that in Honors English," Wanda confirmed. She grabbed a box of tissues from the other side of her desk and slid it in front of Mike.

He took in a deep breath and continued. "Well, my Mom left the state. She may have even left the country; we don't really know." Mike reached out and grabbed a tissue as his eyes glistened from the tears pricking his eyes. He dabbed the sides of his face and continued. "She left him because he was physically, verbally, and mentally abusive towards her."

Wanda chewed the inside of her lip as she sat back in her chair. The black eye was making more sense. Her eyes were filled with sympathy as she scanned Mike's tear-stained face. "Was he also abusive towards you?"

"Verbally, but he was never physically abusive towards me, but he was always physical with her." Mike said before looking down into his lap. He twiddled his thumbs as he played with the ends of his shirt sleeves. Wanda sighed a sigh of relief. Before she could speak again, Mike looked back up, with tears rolling down his face. "Until last night."

Wanda's jaw dropped, and a tear pricked the corner of her eye. "Mike..." she started.

"When I got detention again for cutting up in class," Mike confessed. "He'd had enough."

"Enough of what?"

"Me being a failure, I guess." Mike sniffled and dabbed the corners of his eyes with a new tissue, dropping the other one into the trash can at his feet.

"Mike Kramer, you are not a failure," Wanda said as she leaned forward and brought her head down to look into his eyes. "You are one of the brightest students in this school when you apply yourself."

"It got hard to apply myself after my Mom left." He sobbed. "She was the one who made me feel valued and taken care of. She was nurturing and encouraging. When she left, my life was left with a hole she had once filled."

Wanda closed her eyes and looked away. She thought to her child and how she couldn't fathom having an abusive husband, much less one that put his own child down. What was even more unimaginable for her, however, was having to leave her child behind.

Of course, Mike's mother probably had no choice. It was a small town, as Shawn had so aptly reminded her, and word spread fast amongst faculty and staff when it happened. For her, it was to be killed or get away, and divorce was the only way out. The courts didn't side with her, stating that she was a woman without a job, mentally unstable, and incapable of properly caring for and supporting her son. So, they put Mike in the hands of a monster.

"He used to get mad and verbally abuse me when I would get poor grades, but other than that, he was a decent father-figure to me," Mike continued. "But after the divorce, he blamed me for the divorce. He hated me because I was too much like her. I was rejected by him because he associated me with her all the time. He reminded me that, because of all of this, I would be a failure too."

"Mike," Wanda started, pulling out a tissue and dabbing around the corners of her eyes. "First things first, you're not a failure in my book. You will *never* be a failure in my eyes. Four years ago, I met this outstanding, energetic person—yep, that's you. And guess what? You're still that person, no matter what's happening now. I believe in who you used to be and believe that that young man is still somewhere deep down inside of you. You are going through tough times right now, yes, but these tough times are opportunities learned. You will grow from this and become more powerful than you ever thought you could be." Wanda paused and looked into Mike's eyes. She could see fear in a young man that she never imagined seeing. The fear of a child who was battling for his life. "Tell me something, you're supposed to graduate this year, correct?"

"If I can pass math this semester, yeah."

"You have one class to go, Mike. Finish strong. Graduation is a recognition of all the hard work and dedication you've put in." Wanda brought her head down to be eye level with Mike. "These last few years have been a struggle, but here you are. One class away from graduating. Keep your head up because you've got what it takes to get through this."

"Thank you, Mrs. Hare," Mike said as the fear faded from his eyes and a newfound sense of encouragement replaced it.

"Now, have you any colleges picked out yet?" Wanda asked as she smiled and leaned back in her seat, crossing her legs.

"I'm really leaning towards the University of North Carolina at Wilmington." Mike beamed with pride as he sat up straight.

"That is my alma mater. Maybe I can write you a reference letter." Wanda smiled back at Mike. "Why there?"

"Well," Mike began as he smiled. "I think a change of scenery and to get away from my Dad will be good for me. Plus, none of the guys I'm hanging out with are going to college, so i don't have to worry about getting hung up with them there."

"Not that there is anything wrong with *not* going to college because you can surely make a future for yourself as a tradesman, but I am proud of you for going the college route and pursuing the dreams you have long held onto."

Mike smiled and stood. "I better get going back to detention. I told Mrs. Desmoines that I was going to the bathroom. I should be back by now."

Wanda chuckled and pulled a notebook from her desk drawer. "Wait a minute, Mike, and I will give you a hall pass to give to Mrs. Desmoines."

Mike stopped in his tracks and turned around. With a glistening of joy replacing the glistening of tears in his eyes, Mike smiled at Wanda. "Thank you, Ma'am."

Wanda returned the smile and grabbed a pen, writing a note on the paper and signing it with the flick of her wrist. She handed the note to Mike. "Get going." Mike shook his head and took the piece of paper before leaving the Office and heading back to detention.

Wanda stood and walked to the door, watching as Mike exited the Main Office. She quietly closed her door behind her and walked to the front of her desk. She picked up the phone and dialed a number she hated to know by heart. "Yes, Social Services? I need to report an incident of possible child abuse."

The Friday following Craig's visit, a familiar visitor graced Wanda's office. Peeking her head around the corner of the door, Katherine greeted Wanda. "Mrs. Wanda," Katherine sulked. "Do you have a minute?"

Wanda looked at Katherine, who had her hair in a ponytail with a red scrunchie. Two strands of hair were hanging over Katherine's eyes, and her eyes didn't have the same happiness and curiosity as earlier in the week. Black bags that half mooned the bottom of her eyes and creases in her forehead signaled worry and brought on a pit of anxiety, building like a black hole deep within Wanda's stomach.

After the experience she had just had with Mike, and the way Katherine looked, she was afraid of the worst. "Come in, Katherine," Wanda stammered as she stood and made her way around the desk. Katherine came into the office and closed the door behind her. She walked to where Wanda was standing at the corner of her desk and fell into her arms.

Wanda, slightly surprised, embraced Katherine and wrapped her arms round her. "Are you okay? What's wrong? Did someone hurt you?" Wanda rattled off the questions, unsure of where to start first.

"I'm fine," Katherine sighed, standing back upright. "Well, not really. But I will be."

Wanda quirked an eyebrow and cocked her head to the side. "Please explain."

Katherine turned away from Wanda and walked back towards the door. She reached out and grabbed the door handle. "Never mind, I shouldn't be bothering you with this. It's stupid."

"Katherine," Wanda started as she walked towards her. She reached out and rested her hand on the door. "Nothing that has you like this," she said, waving her hand up and down. "Can be stupid. Talk to me, like you forced Craig to talk to me."

Katherine chuckled at the mention of Craig. She let go of the door handle and turned around. Wanda let go of the door and motioned to a seat. "Now sit," Wanda said as she smirked and made her way back to her chair.

"It's Craig," Katherine started. "It's stupid." She poked her lips out and crossed her arms.

"What do you mean?" Wanda asked with raised eyebrows. She would have thought things were going well between the two of them from the conversation she had with Craig. Mere days ago, they were holding hands and on the verge of confessing their love for one another. "What is going on with Craig?"

"It's what *isn't* going on with Craig that has me annoyed." Katherine huffed and turned her head. "What did he say to you on Monday?"

Wanda chuckled. "Doctor-patient confidentiality." She had felt like a therapist this week, but she didn't mind. She knew she was making a difference in the lives of these students, encouraging them to strive for success in both their personal and professional lives.

Katherine poked her bottom lip out. "That's not fair."

"Ah, but you still haven't told me why you're annoyed with him," Wanda reminded her. "So, who is being unfair, demanding information without giving information?"

Katherine half-smirked at the wittiness of her principal. "I like Craig," she blurted out before clapping her hands over her mouth with bug eyes.

Wanda smiled. "I know."

Katherine's face dropped, and she slouched in her seat. "That obvious, huh?"

Wanda laughed. "You would think, but Craig is clueless."

"How?" Katherine said, as she let out a heavy sigh. "How can he not know? I've done everything short of *tell* him."

"Let me ask you something, Katherine."

Katherine blinked a few times as she contemplated if she was ready for the words that were boiling in Wanda's mouth. "Okay," she said after a moment of hesitation and awkward silence.

Wanda leaned forward and looked into Katherine's eyes. She noticed Katherine was admiring Wanda's bachelor's degree in English literature and education from the University of North Carolina at Wilmington that was hanging on the wall. She was going back to night school to get her master's in educational leadership at Wake Forest University, a short drive from her home.

She looked back at Katherine. "Why haven't you actually told him? You're so willing and ready to give him all the signs, but why are you hesitant to actually tell him you like him?"

"Because." Katherine said as she looked into Wanda's wisdom filled eyes. "It's his job as the boy to tell me. And..."

Wanda squinted her eyes and turned her head slightly to the side. "And?"

The two stared each other down, Wanda daring Katherine to break and reveal the truth while Katherine tried to resist Wanda's compassion and care. "And I think I love him, Mrs. Hare," Katherine finally confessed.

Wanda's face relaxed, and she leaned back in her chair. She clasped her hands together and smiled. "So why exactly is it the boy's job to tell you?"

"That's just the way it has always been, Mrs. Hare. You know that."

"Oh, I do?" Wanda poked her lip out and leaned back, faking hurt from her words. "Because last I checked, it had always been a man's job to be Principal before they offered me the position."

Katherine broke first again as her eyes darted away. Wanda's words had been a snap back to reality for Katherine. "I'm sorry," she whispered.

"Sweetie," Wanda started as she leaned forward and brought her eyes down to meet Katherine's. "Do not be sorry. I am simply making a point that we, as women of power, should constantly challenge the status quo."

Katherine bit her lip and nodded her head. "I know, I just... I'm afraid to tell him. I mean, what if he doesn't feel the same way about me? What if he doesn't like me as more than a friend?"

"Why wouldn't he like you?" Wanda questioned her, staring deeper into her eyes. "You're an intelligent woman, beautiful, and your bubbly personality is infectious. You've really brought down Craig's walls."

She looked away from Wanda'. "Because he's a popular jock and I'm nothing but a loser thespian. I'm unworthy of his love and admiration because I will never be able to give him the status he craves." She confessed.

"Katherine," Wanda said as she closed her eyes and took in a deep breath. She slowly let it out and opened her eyes back up. She smiled at Katherine and took her hand in hers. "Honey, you will never know until you give it a shot. Be the change you wish to see in the world."

Katherine looked up at her and smiled. "Mahatma Gandhi."

"Your first paper you ever wrote for me was an analysis of that quote. You said in there that you wanted to be the change for women to be respected and appreciated, to be revered. You wanted to make a difference in the world, right?" Katherine nodded. "Then be that difference in your own world first. Besides," Wanda paused and smiled at Katherine. "I asked my husband to marry me because I got tired of waiting for him to ask me."

Katherine's eyes lit up, and she beamed with joy. "Do you really think things could work between me and Craig?"

"More than you know, Katherine." Wanda winked at her.

Chapter 11
The Last Week

The first day of the last week of the school year was always an interesting time. Students got restless and unruly as they eagerly counted down the days to summer. Wanda was used to an increase in fights as school year tension boiled over during a time when the punishments were lessened.

Wanda pulled into the parking lot of East Holcomb High in her Mustang. She looked over as Robert unloaded his F-150, taking his briefcase, a lunchbox, and coffee cup. Wanda smiled at Robert when he turned around and saw her. He didn't return the smile but did nod at her as he turned to head for the school's Main Office.

Wanda arched an eyebrow at his demeanor but shook her head as she reached into the passenger seat to gather her purse and briefcase. She paused as her favorite song, *I Will Always Love You,* came on the radio. She smiled as she thought of her husband, George. Through everything she had gone through, George had been the wind beneath her own wings. He was the one that kept her going with his kind words and gentle touch.

She chuckled as she thought about how George was rough and tough on the outside, but deep down, he was a soft teddy bear for his wife. Wanda wondered how she could have gotten so lucky. She hoped to be married to that man for the rest of their lives. "Till death do us part," she whispered to herself.

As Wanda got out of the car, she could hear shouting for help coming from the door to the Main Office. Wanda dropped her stuff in the driver's seat and ran as fast as she could to the sound of Allison's voice. "Allison!" Wanda called out as she rounded the corner.

She saw Allison with panic on her face running toward her. "Wanda! Oh, my goodness, Wanda!" she screamed with fear in her voice.

Wanda met Allison halfway and grabbed Allison by the arms. "What is going on, Allison?"

"Someone left a note on your door."

Wanda waited a minute for Allison to tell her what it said. She cocked her head to the side and squinted her eyes. "Allison," she started as she took a deep breath. "Please tell me what the note says."

"There's a bomb in the school and they're going to detonate it if you come in the building this week," Allison stammered as she spilt the contents of the note. Tears streamed down her face as her breathing quickened and she fell into Wanda.

Wanda's eyes had gone wide, and her silence spoke for itself. She was speechless. In all her time as a teacher and Assistant Vice Principal, she had never experienced a bomb threat. A tear slipped down the corner of her eye as she took in a deep breath. As she exhaled, she said, "Allison, who knows?"

"So far, Robert and you."

Wanda's breath hitched when she found out Robert knew. "What did Robert tell you?"

"To ignore it because it probably wasn't true," she confessed. "He said kids play stupid pranks this time of year."

Wanda sighed and shook her head as she helped Allison off her body. "Allison, here's what I need you to do," Wanda started, closing her eyes. "I'm going home." She opened her eyes. "Call the police. Tell them what's going on. Robert is in charge."

Deep down, Wanda didn't believe there was a bomb in the school. She saw it as a meaningless act of discrimination. She, however, wouldn't take any chances of harming the students and staff that relied on her to keep them safe, so she made the decision to leave until the police could bring in their new bomb sniffing dog.

Secretly, and one she would take to her grave, she wanted to see how Robert would handle the situation. If she wasn't going to be Principal after this year, she wanted to make sure Robert could handle a high-stress situation. It felt wrong to do it, but she knew she had to ensure the students and staff of East Holcomb High were in good hands if-when?-she was fired by the Board at the end of the school year.

"Ar-Are you sure?" Allison stammered.

Wanda closed her eyes and nodded. "This is the way it has to be, Allison." She turned around and opened her eyes. "Be safe, Allison. Call me if you need me." With that, Wanda made her way back to her car.

When she got back to her car, she threw her stuff across the seat. It crashed into the passenger side door. Wanda got in her car and rested her head on the steering wheel. She let loose the swarm of emotion that had been plaguing her mind. She screamed as loud as she could and beat the steering wheel with her fists as tears stained her made up face.

"Pull yourself together, Wanda," she told herself as she lifted her head back up. She reached into her purse and took out the tissues to dab her face. When she had dried her face, she popped the visor down to look at herself in the mirror. "You look like a mess." She sighed and put the car in drive, leaving campus for what she hoped wouldn't be the last time.

When Wanda pulled back up to her house, she swiftly made her way inside, leaving her purse and briefcase slumped against the passenger door. She wanted to call Shawn Carlile as soon as possible and see what Robert had done. She slung open the carport door and power walked towards the phone. Finally, rounding the corner of the kitchen, she took the phone off the receiver and dialed Shawn's office number.

After a few rings, she heard Shawn's strong voice answer the phone. "Shawn Carlile, how can I help you?"

"Shawn," Wanda huffed as she tried to catch her breath. "It's... Wanda... What's the latest... on East Holcomb?"

"What do you mean, Wanda?" George asked as his voice went on high alert. "Why do you sound like you're out of breath? Are you not at the school?"

"No, Shawn," Wanda said as she slumped against the wall in shame and realization. "Someone left a note on my door first thing this morning, before Allison or I made it into the office," Wanda paused, inhaling deeply before exhaling. "It was a bomb threat if I came into the building."

Shawn slammed his fist audibly on his desk. "Why are you just now telling me?"

"I just got home, Shawn," Wanda started, frustrated that Robert hadn't informed the central office. "I couldn't risk going into the building."

"Hold on, Wanda," Shawn grunted. "I have a call coming in."

Wanda waited in silence while Shawn took the other call. Her blood boiled as pieces of the puzzle came together. Everything she had thought before was falling apart. She was so sure of the people who were targeting her, but the strings were unraveling. Slowly, she connected the dots between the person who had complained about her, the person who had thrown a brick through her window, and the person who planted the bomb threat. They were one and the same. She would confront them as soon as it was safe to return to school.

"Wanda," Shawn said as the buzz of silence disappeared, replaced by the man's irritated voice. "I just got a call from the local news media asking about the bomb threat, which I had to answer with 'no comment' because I am *just* now learning about it from you." He paused. "As if that wasn't bad enough, that lovely call was followed by a call from President Thorne. He is *livid* that he did not know before the media.

"Tell me exactly what happened when you found out, Wanda, and speak fast."

"I heard Allison screaming for help," Wanda began as she blinked back the tears. The memory of her screams and seeing her running to her was still etched in her mind, and it was probably one that she would live with for a very long time. "I took off running towards her screams and she ran into me. She told me about the note, the bomb threat, and I instructed what to do and who to leave in charge."

"Who did you leave in charge of the school?" Shawn asked.

"My Assistant Principal, Robert Kane."

Later that evening, Wanda received a phone call from Shawn. "Wanda," he started when she picked up the phone. "First off, I need to apologize."

Wanda raised an eyebrow and shook her head. She was stunned that *she* was the one getting the apology. If anything, she owed Shawn an apology for not having

Allison call the central office as well as the police. "For what, Shawn?"

"I shouldn't have jumped to conclusions with you and been so hostile on the phone earlier," he confessed. "I was shocked, stunned, and scared."

"How do you think I felt, Shawn?" Wanda said as she sniffled. "I was on that campus. I had to leave my students, my staff, behind for their safety."

Shawn was silent for a moment. He exhaled loud enough for Wanda to hear on the other side of the phone. "I can't even imagine. Listen, the bomb dogs came in and searched the entire campus. They didn't find anything on campus, so the police cleared it as a prank. After I found out, I called the school and had Robert evacuate the students."

"Wait a minute," Wanda snapped. "He didn't evacuate the school until *after* I told you?"

"Apparently not," Shawn sighed. "He was reckless and handled this situation poorly. We have suspended Robert for three days without pay."

"So, he'll be back on the last day of school?"

"Yes."

"Thank you, Shawn."

On the last day of school, the door to Wanda's office slung open and slammed into the wall behind it, leaving a hole in the sheetrock. Robert barged into Wanda's office. "You set me up!" he shouted, pointing at Wanda.

Wanda's eyes went wide at the audacity of his accusation. "Just how did you come to this conclusion, Robert?"

Robbert scoffed. "It's an identification. You wanted me out of the picture, so the Board doesn't replace you with me next year," he spat with venom in his voice that paralyzed Wanda in her seat. "I make you feel intimidated. You're not even qualified for the position!"

Wanda blinked rapidly with her jaw agape. She was stunned by this sudden outburst, especially considering everything Wanda had put together. "Robert," she said as she cleared her throat. "Please keep your tone down."

Robert took a deep breath and closed the door behind him. He turned and glared daggers through Wanda's soul. Chills went down Wanda's spine as her body tensed up at the sound of the door latching shut. He walked around to pull a chair closer to Wanda's desk.

"Listen to me, you stupid bitch," Robert spat. "You don't deserve this job, I did. You only got it because you're a woman. A useless woman who should be at home instead of at work." He slammed his fist on the desk. The desk shook and paper fell off the edges. He suddenly shot up and swiped the file organizer off her desk, sending it flying into the wall.

Wanda stood up and pointed her finger at Robert. As she opened her mouth to speak, the door opened slowly, and Allison peeked her head in the door. "Is everything okay in here?" she asked as she looked from Robert to Wanda.

"Everything is fine, Allison," Robert spat as he spun his head to look at her. His breathing was deep as he huffed. "Go back to your office now."

"Do *not* speak to her like that, ever again," Wanda said as she took a step closer to Robert, her finger still pointed directly at his very essence.

Robert looked back at Wanda and shot back, "You're so ungrateful for what you've been given."

"I don't give a rat's ass, Robert, what you think." Wanda said.

"No, Wanda, it's okay. I can leave," Allison said as she shrunk back.

"Stay, Allison." Wanda's eyes never left Robert, even as she spoke those words. "As for you, Robert, since we are throwing accusations, why don't you explain to me why *your* fingerprints were on the brick that was thrown through my window?"

Allison gasped as the words left Wanda's mouth. She stepped into the office and walked towards Wanda. Wanda lowered her arm and looked over at Allison, finally breaking her gaze on Robert. Allison looked over from Wanda to Robert who sat there with a sly smile. "Is that true, Robert?" Allison asked him.

Robert started laughing. "That's preposterous. Someone could have planted the brick after they took it from the school. Weren't there other prints on the brick, Wanda?"

"Yes, that is true." Wanda smiled at him. With a smile, Wanda asked, "How about telling us why *your* truck was seen fleeing my house that night?"

This caused Robert to flinch. He blinked slowly and sat down in the chair. He crossed his arms and squinted his eyes at Wanda. "That's ridiculous."

"My parents witnessed your truck leaving my house when the brick was thrown through the window. They were sitting outside in their sunroom, Robert. They heard the commotion and rushed outside. My wonderful parents who wrote the license plate number down." Wanda pulled out a piece of paper and handed it to him. He snatched the paper and unfolded it, looking down at the license plate number. His face went pale, and his eyes got large. "Which, after looking at your truck in the parking lot Monday, I realized was the same as yours."

"Your parents will say whatever you want them to say. Of course, a judge will throw out their testimony."

"Three additional witnesses identified your truck leaving my house that night around the time the brick was thrown through my window," Wanda confidently stated, crossing her arms and sliding her left foot out.

Robert stood abruptly, knocking the chair into the wall and putting another dent in the sheetrock. Allison flinched and took a step back and away from Robert and Wanda. "Maybe we should all take a deep breath," Allison whispered.

The door slung open, causing Allison to flinch again. All eyes quickly turned towards Coach, who barged into the room. "I heard a commotion coming from the Principal's Office. What's going on in here?"

"I was just telling *Wanda* how useless of a Principal she is," Robert laughed, thinking he had an ally as Wanda had with Allison. "You get it, Coach. She cares more about her image as the first female Principal than she does about this school. I should be the Principal, right?"

Wanda glanced over at Coach. Coach squinted his eyes at her. He suddenly started laughing. "You know what Robert," Coach said as he looked over at Robert. "Had you asked me that nine months ago, I would have agreed with you."

Wanda smiled. Coach was confirming what she had known for the last few days. "You see Robert, when the anonymous complaints came in, I assumed it was Coach because of our disagreements the first week of school.

"Then when the brick was thrown through the window, my husband knew it was a Ford F-150 and once again, I assumed it was Coach because he drives an F-150 and his prints were also on the brick. But you know what they say about assuming," Wanda said as she uncrossed her arms and took a step towards Robert.

Coach grumbled under his breath, "Yeah, it makes an ass out of you."

"Exactly Coach." Wanda chuckled. "You see, I put it together the day I talked to Shawn Carlile, and he told me you never called the Central Office. You were angry that I had told Allison to call the police. Your intention was to keep it hush-hush, so you could be in control this week and pretend I was skipping.

"Good guess, but wrong," Robert said.

"Actually," Wanda said as her finger shot up in the air to silence him. "I believe I am right on target. In fact, I think you even wrote the bomb threat against the school."

Allison gasped and her eyes went wide as she looked at Robert with disgust and fear in her eyes. "Robert..."

"You're going crazy, Wanda," Robert said as he shook his head and started towards the door.

Coach stepped in front of the door and crossed his arms. "Start answering questions, Kane."

"You see, Robert," I had the Science Lab run a test on the fingerprints to see if they matched the fingerprints from the brick. Your fingerprints. I didn't tell them who the fingerprints belonged to or where they came from, but they got a match."

"I started having suspicions around the time of the fight that happened at the beginning of the year that put me in the hospital," Wanda admitted. "I watched you watch me laying there, bleeding on the floor. You walked away without helping. But I still couldn't shake the thought of it being Coach."

"Okay," Coach said as he leaned over and looked around Robert to Wanda. "Can we stop mentioning that?"Wanda smiled softly and nodded at him. "Of course, last time I will mention it," she said. "Then, you undermined me in front of the group of boys that I caught smoking in the boys' bathroom. Something about that made me realize you weren't really on my side like you had tried to make it seem. You wanted the position for yourself."

Robert bit his lip and looked from Coach, to Allison, to Wanda, and finally sighed and hung his head. "Fine," he looked up at Wanda. "I filed the anonymous complaints, trying to get you fired so I could take over and get what I rightfully deserve. Yes, I threw the damn brick through your window, hoping you would leave town and I would finally be rid of you. I planted the bomb threat to get you to leave school so I could prove I was a better Principal than you.

"I was jealous of you, you stupid bitch. But it's because I would be a better Principal and everyone in this room knows it."

"Actually," Coach said with a grunt. "I think she's the best damn thing to happen to Holcomb County Schools."

"Me too," Allison said. "Best damn thing to happen to Holcomb County schools, if you ask me."

"Nobody asked any of you," Robert shouted as he threw his arms up in the air. "Move, Coach, or I will write you up for subordination."

Coach laughed as he stepped to the side. Robert glared at him as he walked past Coach. He stopped as he went to close the door behind him and turned his head to the side. "I *will* have your job one day, Wanda." With those words, he left the room and closed the door behind him.

Wanda sighed and collapsed in her chair. "Thank you both," she said to Coach and Allison. She looked over at the phone and said, "Was that enough?"

"I sent my men about five minutes ago," said Sheriff Grant in a somber tone. "He'll be in cuffs before the end of the hour."

"I'm shocked," followed Shawn Carlile's voice, also on the line.

Chapter 12
The First Last Day

Wanda sat with her head buried in her desk. This school year had been a lot for her, mentally and physically. She had found herself not sleeping because of the anxiety of what would happen the next day at school. Sometimes she was afraid of every slight movement outside her house for fear of another, perhaps worse, attack on her family. Even moments when she would wake up with nightmares of something terrible happening to Michelle because of her.

She knew that Robert's outburst, his anger that coursed through his veins and spilled out through his actions, would haunt her memory for a very long time. It was a moment in time she would be forced to relive repeatedly in her nightmares.

Despite the fear that had iced her veins, Wanda was proud of herself for remaining strong and steadfast in the face of his anger. She was scared, that was for sure. She had heard horror stories, one of them being from Mike Kramer, about what a man who thinks he is superior to women will do to prove his point. Before today, she never would have guessed Robert could be that kind of person, but this proved that you could never be too careful with who you put your trust in.

It was painful to watch the police take Robert away in handcuffs. Robert and she had been friends for years before she accepted the Principal position, so him being the one to turn on her the quickest was a shock. Seeing him in the shiny bracelets clasped around both wrists was even more shocking than that. In fact, it made her wonder just who she could trust.

Maybe she had valid reasons to hesitate towards Shawn in the initial stages. Not because he was guilty, but because you can never be sure who to trust when you are a woman in power. Anyone could be out to get you at any moment. After everything he had done for her, though, Wanda knew she could count on Shawn now.

Even more surprising was the fact that Coach had come around. Admittedly, when she had approached Coach with the plan to trick Robert into confessing his crimes, she wasn't sure if he would be on her side. Again, she couldn't be too sure of whom to put her trust in anymore. However, something told her Coach would come around when he found out it would help clear his name from the list of suspects.

Then there was Allison. Allison had been by her side since East Holcomb's first day under her leadership. When she approached Allison to come in as a witness, she didn't expect her to be a target of Robert's anger. Allison was brave, however, despite her timid demeanor and would follow Wanda through hellfire and back if it came down to it.

She lifted her head up and looked over at the clock ticking away at the minutes until 3:00. Her phone rang, and she looked down as the number for the Central Office flashed across her screen. She smiled as she went to answer the phone call from Shawn Carlile.

A much younger version of Shawn Carlile made his way into Wanda's classroom. He looked around as Wanda took down

the various posters her class had created as part of their projects. Wanda, feeling the presence of someone standing in the doorway of her classroom, turned around to see Shawn standing there.

He ran a finger across his dark mustache and smiled. "Wanda," he started as he made his way into the room. "I wanted to let you know your classes received the highest averages in the history of the English department."

Wanda ran a hand through her wavy black hair. "Are you serious, Shawn?"

"As a heart attack," Shawn confirmed.

Wanda sat down at a student desk beside her and propped her chin up with her fists. "I didn't expect them to do that well," she admitted. "I believe all my students have the potential to achieve success, but you know how it is, Shawn. Ultimately, it's up to the student to pursue success."

"While that's true in a sense, Wanda," Shawn started as he made his way to the desk in front of her, then sat down and turned around backwards in the chair to face Wanda before he continued. "I have always been a firm believer that it's the catalyst that is the most important part of the explosion.

"The catalyst plays a crucial role in the process of an explosion: It acts as a trigger, initiating and accelerating the reaction, transforming a relatively stable system into a highly energetic and volatile one," Shawn explained to her. "The significance of the catalyst lies in its ability to lower the activation energy required for the reaction to occur, making it more accessible and efficient. Without the catalyst, the reaction

would either not occur or proceed at an extremely slow rate. Thus, the catalyst is the key component that determines the speed, intensity, and success of an explosion."

Slightly confused by the scientific explanation coming from a former science teacher, Wanda arched an eyebrow and leaned back in her chair. "What exactly does that mean in terms of the students' success, Shawn?"

Shawn chuckled. "Similarly, teachers can act as catalysts to ignite their students' potential," Shawn began again. "They are the key figures who can lower the barriers and obstacles that prevent their students from reaching their potential. Teachers can help students grow and develop by providing support and guidance. They can create a conducive learning environment that promotes curiosity, creativity, and critical thinking, making learning engaging and enjoyable.

"Teachers can also recognize their students' strengths, weaknesses, and interests, tailoring the curriculum and activities to their unique needs and preferences. By doing so, they can unleash their students' potential, transforming them into highly energetic and enthusiastic learners."

"So," Wanda said as she stroked her chin and thought about what Shawn was saying. "Teachers can act as catalysts in igniting their students' potential, by making the students the most important component in the educational process."

Shawn smiled and pointed at her. "Exactly. And you've got it, Wanda."

"What is it, Shawn?" Wanda questioned with a raised eyebrow.

"The innate and raw desire to shape the lives of these students," he told her. *"Everything you do, you push these students to be better. From day one, when you jumped up on the desk and acted out a Shakespearean scene, the students admired you. You showed them learning could be fun. Showed them their own potential."*

"Well, Shawn, my goal of becoming a teacher was to make a difference in the lives of the students," Wanda admitted. *"It surely wasn't for the pay."*

Shawn laughed and leaned back against the desk. *"Nobody gets into teaching for the pay, but some* do *get into it for the benefits. You. You though, you're different Wanda. You want to make things better for the students so that they can, in turn, become the best versions of themselves."*

Wanda looked down and away. *"Is it always this hard, Shawn?"* Wanda finally asked after a moment of silence shared between the two.

"What? Teaching?"

"Being responsible for the future." Wanda looked back at Shawn. He could see the fatigue in her eyes, the black bags that had cupped the bottom of her eye, and the wrinkles forming in her forehead. A line of grey had formed around her ear, perfectly rounding it.

Shawn frowned. *"It doesn't get easier, that's for sure,"* Shawn admitted with a sigh. *"But Wanda, you have so much potential to make a difference in this school district, and in this world. You're a different type of educator. You carry a fiery passion I haven't ever seen in my ten years of school experience."*

"Why?"

Shawn slightly turned his head and squinted his eyes at Wanda. "Why, what?"

"Why did you hire me?" Wanda asked him as she looked deep into his gaze.

"Easy," Shawn smiled, his mustache capping it off. "You're going to be the best damn thing to ever happen to Holcomb County Schools and I wanted to take credit for that hire. I figured it would look good on my resume when I work my way up to Superintendent." He winked at Wanda and Wanda laughed.

"I could definitely see you being a fantastic Superintendent one day," Wanda smiled softly.

"First black superintendent would be a wonderful way to leave my legacy on this world," Shawn confessed. "Do you have children, Wanda?" Shawn asked her.

Wanda slowly shook her head. "Not yet," she said. "My husband and I married a few years ago and we're looking at having kids in the next year or so."

"They're truly a blessing, Wanda," Shawn started with a smile sprawled across his face. "I have two. Jerome and Jane." Shawn paused and took a deep breath. "We were pregnant once before either of them were born. My wife - then girlfriend - was 19 and I was 21. We were young kids in love, not nearly ready for a child but prepared to take one on." A tear slipped

out of the corner of Shawn's eye and he blinked back the flood of emotion welling up in his eyes.

Wanda got up and made her way to her desk at the front of the room. When she got there, she grabbed the box of tissues she kept for students going through tough times and took it to where she and Shawn were sitting.

Shawn nodded with a smile and took a tissue to dab his eyes. "Thank you," he said. "She was born August 19th, 1968. I missed my first first day of teaching because my wife went into labor that morning when we woke up." Shawn paused again and his eyes went blank as he stared through Wanda. "I held baby Michelle Carlile in my arms for about one minute before I realized she stopped breathing." Shawn let one arm rest on the desk as he brought his other fist to his teeth and bit them.

Wanda gasped as a tear slipped from her eye. Her heart sank at the mere thought of losing a baby, much less holding them and then losing them. She reached out and placed her hand on his. "You don't have to say any more, if you don't want to, Shawn."

"The doctors didn't want to help us because we were black," Shawn said through clenched teeth. "They would rather have watched my baby die than believe the word of an 'uneducated negro.'"

Wanda hung her head and gently shook it in shame for how someone had treated one of the kindest men she knew in such a time of need. "How can people be so cruel?"

Shawn slowly let his eyes drift back to meet Wanda's worried gaze. He gently smiled at her, so gently Wanda almost didn't notice it. "People aren't cruel, they're jealous. People are jealous of other people's success. Of their beauty. Of their uniqueness. They live miserable lives and try to bring everyone down with them.

"While it was a painful part of my past, losing Michelle made me clean up some bad habits and get on the right track. I eventually married Maureen six months later, quit drinking a year later, and put down cigarettes for good a year and a half later.

"We got our lives together and work on creating our best selves before we tried having kids again. Both because we weren't ready to have kids yet and we weren't ready to go through the heartbreak of losing another child. It was one of the best things we ever did because I could give Jerome and Jane a life worth living, struggle free.

"I want to leave my mark for Michelle and inspire Jerome and Jane. I want to show them that just because they are a different color than most of the surrounding people, they can still be successful and are still worthy of love. Black is beautiful."

"Yes," Wanda smiled. "Yes, it is."

"Hello, Shawn," Wanda said as she answered the phone. "Ready for your vacation?"

Shawn chuckled from the other end of the line. "As I'll ever be," Shawn said. "You know how it is with kids and summer break. It's nice to have a break from work, but sometimes you just want a break from the kids."

Wanda laughed. "How are Jane and Jerome doing?"

"They are as restless as always." Shawn sighed. "Jerome barely passed his science class, but he is excelling at football. I couldn't believe *my* son would almost fail a science class." He laughed. "Jane is my bookworm. In fact, she has been so inspired by you and your journey this last year that she is considering a career in teaching. She has been doing a lot of schoolwork preparing for college, and her top choice is Wake Forest, because of your decision to go there for your Masters."

"That time already?" Wanda asked, trying to calculate their ages.

Shawn let out a chuckle. "Not quiet," he said. "Jane will be a sophomore next year, but she is already looking at colleges. Jerome will be a freshman, thankfully." He paused and cleared his throat. "How is Michelle?"

"Well," Wanda started as she clicked her tongue. "Michelle will make her way to middle school next year, so I am expecting a bit of anxiety to form within her this summer. Like mother, like daughter, after all."

"If that little girl ends up being anything like her mother," Shawn said. "She'll be one hell of a woman.

Thank you again for naming her after my little angel baby."

"Thank *you*, Shawn," Wanda started with a smile. "For always believing in me."

"You're following in my footsteps, Wanda." Shawn said.

"What do you mean?" Wanda raised an eyebrow.

"After six years as a teacher, they promoted me to the first black Assistant Principal in the school district. After seven years of teaching, you were the first female Assistant Principal in our school district," Shawn explained. "After three years, I received a promotion to Principal. Three years for you, too."

Wanda laughed. "So, you intend to retire in nine years so I can become the first female Superintendent?"

Shawn was silent. "Maybe even sooner."

"What do you mean, Shawn?" Wanda said with a gasp.

"I've got about five or so more years left before I can step back and into a consultancy role for a couple of years to retire with state benefits. I won't be Superintendent for the full ten years of my forties. I'm going to take some time when my kids graduate to travel with my wife." Shawn said. "That's why one of my stipulations for hiring you was for you to go back and get your masters."

"You *really* want me to take your role when you retire, don't you?" Wanda asked. Her jaw hung in disbelief. She had just become Principal, and already Shawn had believed enough in her to want her to be Superintendent after him.

Shawn chuckled on the other side of the phone. Wanda, your incredible first year as Principal shattered academic records. I can't even begin to imagine what you could accomplish as Superintendent."

"Shawn," Wanda started. She paused, struggling in her search for the right words. "Do you really think there is any hope in the next five years that we will get a Board that would even remotely *consider* a female Superintendent, much less actually hire one?"

"I think you've swayed a lot of opinions, Wanda."

"I highly doubt Henry Thorne has changed his mind at this point." Wanda sighed and thought back to the pounding gavel of President Thorne during her Board meeting performance review. "Despite everything I said, despite all the evidence against the claims, he never wavered in his disgust for me during that meeting."

"People can change their mind, Wanda," Shawn reminded her. "Who would have thought ten years ago when you started that they ever would have hired a black Superintendent? But they did it this year. We both transcended the boundaries of our wildest dreams."

Chapter 13

Graduation

"I stand before you today, honored to represent the graduating class of 1987," Katherine Church started. "We have come a long way and have achieved so much during our time at East Holcomb High School. Today, we celebrate the end of one chapter and the beginning of another. However, before we move forward, I would like to take a moment to recognize a trailblazing woman who has made history in our community." She smiled and looked to her left at Wanda. Wanda smiled at her and nodded, fighting back a tear.

"Principal Wanda, your appointment as the first female Principal in Holcomb County history is a testament to your unwavering dedication to education and your commitment to breaking barriers," Katherine continued. "You have inspired and empowered all of us as Panthers to think beyond the limitations that society has placed on us. Your leadership has set an example for future generations, and we are forever grateful for the impact you have made on our lives." A few students in the crowd let out cheers and whoops at Katherine's words. Katherine smiled.

"As we move forward," Katherine said, as she looked back at the crowd. "Let us remember the lessons we have learned both inside and outside the classroom. Let us carry the values of hard work, perseverance, and determination into our future endeavors. And let us never forget the memories we have made together, from singing along to Whitney Houston's I *Wanna Dance with Somebody* to quoting lines from "The Princess Bride." The students laughed as they thought back to school dances, late-night bonfires, and all their other wonderful experiences throughout their high school years.

Katherine continued, "As we go out into the world, let us be confident in our abilities, and let us strive to make our dreams a reality. I have no doubt that each and every one of us will go on to achieve great things and make a difference in our communities." Katherine paused as she stared out across the sea of students. Her eyes landed on Craig and their eyes locked. She smiled at him and he blushed, but returned her smile.Kather ine turned back to look at Wanda. "So, on behalf of the class of 1987, I would like to thank you, Principal Wanda, for your leadership, your guidance, and your unwaver- ing commitment to our education. Congratulations to my fellow graduates and may we all find success and happiness in the years to come.

"Thank you." The crowd erupted in applause as most of the student section shot out of their seat clapping and whooping at the excellent speech Katherine had just given. She walked off the stage and Wanda took her place.

"Dear Graduates," Wanda started, smiling across the crowd. Her eyes landed on Katherine and Craig, sitting beside each other with their hands intertwined. She smiled and continued. "As the first female Principal in Holcomb County Schools, I am honored to stand before you today. This day marks the culmination of years of hard work, dedication, and determination. I know firsthand the obstacles that many of you have had to overcome in order to reach this point. But let me tell you, your perseverance has paid off." A few of the students clapped and Wanda smiled at them.

"I want you to know that you are capable of achieving more than you ever thought possible," Wanda said with confidence in her voice. She glanced in the front row of the crowd and spotted both George dressed in a suit and Michelle in a cute salmon dress with white frills. She smiled at her daughter who in return waved and shouted, "Hey, Mommy!"

The crowd chuckled and Wanda laughed, shaking her head. Wanda paused and looked beside her at Shawn Carlile and Henry Thorne. "You have the power to push beyond the limits that others have set for you. You have the power to shatter glass ceilings and break down barriers. You have the power to make a difference in this world."

Wanda turned back to the crowd. "As you move forward from this day, I encourage you to embrace your strengths, to never give up, and to always keep pushing forward. Remember that failure is not an end, but a beginning. It is an opportunity to learn, to grow, and to become better."

Wanda glanced at Katherine and Katherine smiled at her. "In the words of Whitney Houston's "I Wanna Dance with Somebody," "Don't you wanna dance, say you wanna dance, don't you wanna dance." Yes, you do. You want to dance through life, to embrace all of the challenges and triumphs that come your way. You want to be like Buttercup in "The Princess Bride," to face obstacles with courage and conviction, and to emerge victorious." The crowd let out a chuckle and Wanda winked at Katherine. Katherine gave her a thumbs up.

"So, graduates," Wanda continued. "I congratulate you on this momentous occasion. I am proud of each and every one of you, and I have no doubt that you will go on to achieve great things. Remember that you are capable of more than you ever thought possible. Keep pushing, keep striving, and never give up.

"Thank you."

After graduation, Wanda stood on the stage waiting for the crowd to clear out. She looked out amongst the crowd with a smile. She saw Michelle and George waiting off to the side with a bouquet of roses. Her favorite flower. She moved towards the steps closest to Michelle and George.

Before she could get very far, an eerily familiar voice called out, "Wanda?"

Wanda closed her eyes and turned around. "President Thorne," Wanda said with a smile and a nod. "Thank you for being here today."

President Henry Thorne cleared his throat and nodded at her. "Of course," he said. "It is my duty, after all."

He let out a hardy laugh. "However, I do owe you an apology."

Wanda's eyes went wide, and she brought her head back abruptly. "I'm sorry?"

"I was too harsh on you at the Board Meeting review," he admitted, hanging his head. "If I would have known Robert Kane was behind everything, I never would have..."

"Mr. Thorne, it's fine." Wanda said. She was quietly biting her tongue. What she really wanted to say was that he shouldn't have been as hard on her even if he didn't know Robert was behind it because there was no evidence or anything to support the baseless claims.

"The school ended with the highest marks in the history of the school district." The Board President looked up at Wanda. "Maybe everyone was right."

Wanda cocked her head to the side and raised an eyebrow. "What do you mean?"

"So many people, including Shawn Carlile, have told me something that I never believed." He paused. "You're the best damn thing to happen to Holcomb County Schools."

Wanda blushed with a smile and glanced down and away. "Thank you, Mr. Thorne."

He nodded and said, "I need to get going. West Holcomb is having their graduation in an hour." He paused and cleared his throat again. "Anyway, thank you for being the best damn thing to happen to Holcomb County

Schools." He turned around and walked away. As Wanda turned around, intending to approach George and Michelle, Shawn came forward to greet her.

"What was that about?" Shawn asked as he got closer to Wanda.

Wanda smiled. "He apologized for the way he acted at the Board Meeting," she said with disbelief. Even though she had heard everything with her own ears, she still had a hard time believing that someone who had been so vehemently against her had apologized. "He even said I was the best damn thing to happen to Holcomb County Schools."

Shawn smiled. "Sounds like you really are making waves in Holcomb County."

"And finally, some good waves," Wanda laughed.

Shawn laughed back and put a hand on Wanda's shoulder. "In case no one has told you lately, I'm proud of you, Wanda."

"For what, Shawn?"

"For being so strong and overcoming the adversity," Shawn said with a twinkle in his eye. "And for helping us figure out it was Robert behind everything. I'm still in disbelief."

"Me too, Shawn," Wanda said, shaking her head. "I really thought I would have you and Robert on my side, at the very least," she admitted. "Robert and I were close when we were both Assistant Principals."

"You're a Principal with principles, Wanda," Shawn smiled. "You're one of a kind. Don't you ever forget that." Shawn looked to Wanda's left and back at Wanda. "I think you have a couple of visitors. I'll let you get to them."

Wanda, thinking George and Michelle had snuck up on her, turned around to see Craig and Katherine coming up to her, hand in hand. "Principal Wanda!" Katherine shouted as she let go of Craig's hand and ran to Wanda. When Katherine got to her, she wrapped Wanda in a warm embrace. Wanda laughed and wrapped her arms around Katherine.

"Please, call me Wanda now," Wanda said.

Katherine shook her head "Yes, Wanda."

"That was a beautiful speech you gave, Katherine," Wanda said as the two left their embrace. Craig had finally caught up to Katherine. Katherine took a step back and took Craig's hand in hers.

"Thank you, Ma'am," Katherine said with a blush. She looked over at Craig and back at Wanda. "For everything. For being an inspiration to not just me, but to the entire school. For showing me what a woman was capable of. Not only that…" she trailed off with her face reddening and looked away.

Craig looked over at her and back at Wanda. "Well, you see Wanda…" Craig cleared his throat. "We started dating."

Wanda smiled at the young love and asked, "That's great, you two."

Craig smiled, "Yeah, after both of us talked to you about how we were feeling about the other, Katherine finally had the guts to confess her love for me first."

Wanda smiled as Katherine looked at her. She winked at Katherine and Katherine smiled back. "I figured if you could ask your husband, I could ask Craig," Katherine admitted. "You've inspired me more than you will ever know."

"Where are you two going to college?" Wanda asked the couple.

"University of North Carolina at Wilmington," they said in unison.

"We're going to major in education, to follow in your footsteps," Katherine explained.

"Your alma mater," Craig said with a beaming smile.

Wanda was stunned that they knew that, but as many times as they had been in her office, she shouldn't have been. "I'm proud of both of you, you know that?" Both smiled and nodded. Wanda held her arms out, and the pair embraced her hug.

"We've got to get going," Katherine chirped as they released their embrace once more. "We're meeting each other's parents at lunch today!"

Wanda raised her eyebrows and smiled. "Good luck."

"Thanks!" they both called out and turned around to leave.

Wanda smiled and turned around to head towards the steps to see her husband and daughter. When she got to the steps and walked down them, Mike appeared from her right.

"Principal Wanda?" He called as he took a step towards her. He had cut his hair down to a high and tight fade and was wearing his graduation robe. "I just wanted to tell you thank you."

"For what, Mike?" Wanda said as she turned her head to the side.

"Always being on my side and believing in me," he said. He looked from side to side and back at Wanda. "I do have a question, though."

"Yes?"

"Did you call Social Services on my Dad after I talked to you?" he asked.

Wanda's heart quickened. She had heard what happened to Mike's Dad. After she had talked to Social Services and they did an investigation, they reopened his abuse claims filed by his ex-wife. They found him guilty on multiple counts of spousal and child abuse. "I had to, by law, Mike," Wanda began. "I'm sorry about what happened to your Dad, and I hope one day you'll forgive me."

"I'm not mad at you," he said with a confused look written across his face.

"You're not?" Wanda asked.

"No," he said. "When they took my Dad away, my Mom came back. I've been staying with her ever since. I even made the high honor roll the second semester because of her." Mike let a tear slip down his cheek. "Wanda, you changed my life," Mike continued. "You made me believe I was better than what my Dad told me I was. You helped me get my Mom back. Because of you, I did this. And I can never repay you for that."

"I'm so proud of you, Mike, but you did this, not me. I was simply the catalyst that put it into action. You were the driving force and the winner of this game of life. You chose to be better and be more. I simply believed in you. I believe in all my students because I know each and every one of them is capable of whatever they want to accomplish."

Wanda opened her arms and embraced Mike with a hug. "And college?" She let go and leaned back.

"I got accepted to UNCW," he said with beaming pride shining in his eyes. "Thanks to you and pushing me to do better, I joined the debate club my last semester and I think that extracurricular was what won them over for me. Of course, I'm sure your recommendation letter was a nice cherry on the top."

"Mike?" A female's voice called out. Wanda looked over at a blonde woman approaching them.

Mike looked over and back at Wanda. "Principal Wanda," Mike said as the woman approached. "This is my mother, Patricia."

"You're the one who helped save me and my son," Patricia said as she put an arm around Mike and hugged him to the side.

"I don't know about all that," Wanda said. "I was just doing my job."

"Doing your job or not," Patricia said when she looked over at Mike. "You saved Mike. You saved me. You saved our family. I will always be grateful to you for that."

Wanda blinked to hold back tears. Everyone's words were becoming overwhelming emotional. It wasn't that she didn't appreciate them, it was just that she didn't want to break down in front of all these people. She sniffled and smiled at Patricia and Mike. "I need to go see my husband and daughter, but it was a pleasure to meet you, Patricia." Wanda extended her hand and Patricia shook it.

Wanda then passed by on her way to George and Michelle. Michelle looked up from the ground and saw Wanda approaching. She let go of George's hand to run to Wanda and he reached out for her, but she was too quick. When she got to her Mom, she jumped up and Wanda caught her to bring her into a bear hug. "I love you, my Munchkin," Wanda said into Michelle's head. She kissed the top of her head.

"I love you too, Mommy," Michelle whispered, as she nuzzled her head under Wanda's chin.

"'Chelle Hare!" George called out when he caught up to her. "Yous knows better than to run away like tha'!"

Michelle leaned back in her Mom's arms and looked at her wide-eyed. Wanda mouthed 'I got this' to her, and she smiled. "George," Wanda said as she put Michelle down. "You look handsome in that suit."

Instantly George's face went from a brown tint to a maroon tint as his cheeks reddened. "Well thank ya, Ma'am. Tha' wassa good speech ya gave up ther'." George smiled and took her hand in his. He brought her hand to his lips and placed a gentle kiss in the middle of her hand.

"Thank you, George," Wanda giggled as she looked away with a smile. "You helped me so much during this journey. I wouldn't have been able to survive this without your strength and support."

"Suppor', maybe," George laughed. "Strength, tha's all you, hon."

"What do you mean?" she asked him.

"You one of tha stronges' women-no, person-I know." George stepped towards his wife and brought her in for a hug.

In her husband's embrace, she let the tears flow. It had been a long and emotional rollercoaster in her first year as the Principal at East Holcomb High. She knew it was worth it, but she just didn't know how strong she was. She wasn't sure, from day one, whether she could handle the job.

But, she'd done it. She defied expectations and achieved what others believed she couldn't. Her actions disproved the doubts of others, leading to the formation of new alliances and the creation of new enemies. She had discovered a dark truth that had haunted her all year, but she had overcome it all to lead the school to the highest marks in Holcomb County Schools history.

George gently rubbed her back as she soaked the front of his suit with her tears. He gently kissed the top of her head and whispered, "Shhh... I gotcha."

Michelle pulled on the side of Wanda's robe. Wanda looked down at her daughter and smiled. "Hi, Honey."

"What's wrong, Mommy?" Michelle asked with furrowed eyebrows. "Why are you crying?"

"'Chelle, she's fine," George said as he looked down at his daughter.

"No," Wanda said as she let go of George and knelt to face her daughter. "Mommy isn't okay, and Michelle needs to know it's okay not to be okay."

George put his hand on his wife's shoulder. "Are you sure, Hon?"

Wanda looked up at him and bit her lip, nodding gently. She turned back to face Michelle. "Honey, Mommy has this thing called anxiety," Michelle furrowed her eyebrows again and turned her head to the side. "It means I worry about things a lot, more powerfully than most people do. I feel more than other people do and Mommy faced a lot of mean people during her first year as Principal."

"Like the boy who called you the b-word?" She asked, her eyes dropping with sadness.

"Just like him," Wanda said. "In fact, his Daddy, Robert, was one of the worst."

"I'm sorry, Mommy," Michelle said as she sniffled back a tear. "Why are people mean?"

"Most of the time, they are just jealous of other people," Wanda explained. "Some people like to put others down as a way to lift themselves up for a moment in time. The thing is, they always go back down to being miserable because they'll never be happy with themselves."

"I'm sorry you have anonymity, Mommy," Michelle sniffled out.

George and Wanda both let out a little laugh. "'Xiety honey," George said, trying his level best to correct his daughter.

"*An*xiety, Honeys," Wanda laughed as she stood up. "And it's okay, because God gave it to me to help me become stronger. Michelle, I want you to always remember what you are capable of. Don't ever let anyone make you feel you are a lesser person just because you are a woman.

"You are powerful, strong, and independent. You will always survive, no matter what life throws at you along the way. God has made us *all* in his image. He has a plan for us, and for as long as we love and live like He did, we will survive. That and the love of each other. Always remember that you are not alone in this life."

Michelle smiled and hugged her mom and dad's legs. "I love you, Mommy; I love you, Daddy." Wanda and George wrapped linked arms with Michelle in the middle of them. "Where are we going, Mommy?" Michelle asked as she looked up at Michelle.

"Toa pig pickin,'" George smiled down at her.

Photo by Sarah Peterson

Retiring Bolivia Elementary principal Sue Sellers clears her desk after 33 years in public education.

THE PRINCIPAL'S PRINCIPLES

F or Sue Sellers, retirement is bittersweet
Teacher, principal never doubted her role throughout 33 years in public education

- **By Sarah Peterson**, Staff Writer, The State Port Pilot, July 7th, 2004

Ending her 33-year career at Bolivia Elementary School was fitting for Sue Sellers. The principal attended the same school as a young student and then later came back as a teacher.

"I don't think there was a doubt," she said about returning to her native Brunswick County. "It was something I thought I should do. The school system gave me so much, and was my opportunity to give back."

Last Wednesday, Sellers sat at her mostly cleared desk in a corner of the school's library. The offices are getting a facelift for the summer.

"It's bittersweet," she said on her final day. "I'm excited. But when you've done something for 33 years, it's hard to walk out because you'll never come back."

Between rounds of golf and spending time with her family, she still plans to be involved with education.

"I'm not sure how yet – maybe as a volunteer," Sellers said. "It will always be an interest. My heart will always b in Bolivia and South Brunswick (High School)."

Teaching was a natural choice for Sellers, but it wasn't her first. After attending Bolivia Elementary from first grace through high school, she attended UNC-Wilmington.

"I started as a journalism major," she said. "Then I decided early on that I really wanted to be a teacher."

A roster of wonderful teachers at Bolivia and family commitment to education brought her into the field.

"Teaching was a highly regarded profession in my family," she said. "My parents always had such respect for my teachers. If I had to do it over again, I would choose the same thing – I would go into education."

In the beginning

Sellers' first year was at Waccamaw. The next year she was back at Bolivia High School, teaching English.

"I remember dismissing early because tobacco farmers had to do tobacco crops," she said. "We also didn't have workdays. We managed to get it all done."

The next year, though, there was no early dismissal for farming, and the teachers were given a few workdays

It was also her second year that South Brunswick High School opened, and Bolivia house graces 1-8.

The new school consolidated the upper graces from both Bolivia and Southport High School.

"That was quite intense," Sellers recalled. "The first year, it was 'us' and 'them'. We had to mesh the two cultures – beach and rural – but it didn't take long."

She was the first English department chair at South Brunswick and also coached basketball.

Sellers spent 24 years of her career at the high school – first as a teacher, then as assistant principal and finally as principal.

"My mentor made sure I knew everything about administration," she said. "he pushed me to go to grad school. The hard thing was becoming an assistant principal. I had been a teacher, and I was no longer one of them."

After eight years at the helm of South Brunswick, she was transferred to Bolivia, where he grandsons would become the fourth generation to attend the school.

Making the jump from the classroom to an administrative position did not compare to switching gears from high school to elementary school.

"You can't imagine," Sellers said. "My mind was high school. I never envisioned being an elementary principal. It was quite different but a neat way to end my career."

Understanding the challenges of high school, she said, helped her become a better principal at the elementary level.

"What happens in elementary school makes a difference for the rest of their life, as far as education," she said. "If they had a different experience in elementary school, they may have done better in high school. Every level is important, but this is where these little guys get their start."

Changes in education

"The kids have truly not changed," Sellers said.

Federal mandates, though, have forced an education evolution on schools, which has not necessarily been for the better.

"It is difficult for teachers and administrators to truly do what's best for the children with all these federal mandates," she said. "People look at us as an industry with quality control. We're not an industry. We're dealing with human beings, with children."

The federal No Child Left Behind Act is the latest obstacle for education.

"I fully adree that no child should be left behind," she said. "This has been one of the most frustrating things for me these last few years."

Even so, teaching is a very rewarding career. Sellers said she tells young teachers not to focus so much on their salary.

"When one of your students writes you a note thanking you for being tough on them and helping them, there isn't enough money in the world to replace that."

For teachers she leaves behind, Sellers wants them to always put the students first.

"That's why we're here," she said. "You help them become the best possible person they can be – and not just academically."

As she prepared to leave her desk and post behind, Sellers scanned the shelves of books around her.

"If I did a bar graph of my 33 years, the positives would be way, way up high," she said, reaching into the air with her arm. "The negatives would be one of those tiny things at the bottom you can barely see. It's been good."

Tyler Wittkofsky, a literary dynamo from North Carolina, conquered addiction and undiagnosed mental illness in college, emerging as the President of Tea With Coffee Media. A versatile professional with award-winning marketing skills, he deftly navigates multiple genres as an author, blogger, and podcaster. Tyler's journey, marked by resilience, is reflected in his debut poetry collection, "Coffee, Alcohol, and Heartbreak," and novels like "(Not) Alone" and "The

Seeds of Love: Sunflower Kisses Book One." His literary prowess extends to anthologies, online magazines, and insightful contributions to www.TylerWittkofsky.com. Co-founding Tea With Coffee Media in 2022, Tyler champions indie voices, fostering a diverse storytelling landscape. His impact resonates not just in literature but also through podcasts like Back Porch Parley and Cook the Books. Tyler and his wife Grace embark on enchanting adventures chronicled in the blog Adventure With Coffee, inviting readers to share in the magic of their nomadic journey.

Other Works

(Not) Alone
A Mental Health Novella

Coffee, Alcohol, and Heartbreak:
A Poetry Collection

The Sunflower Kisses Series
A Man's POV Romance

Book 1: The Seeds of Love

TYLER WITTKOFKSY

Enamored Echoes (with Kelsey Anne Lovelady)
Romantic Fantasy Series

Book 1: Potent